SEAL
OF APPROVAL

JACK SILKSTONE

VINCI
BOOKS

SEAL
OF APPROVAL

JACK SILKSTONE

VUCI
BOOKS

This book is dedicated to the Military Working Dogs who have served, loyal and steadfast, alongside their handlers in the world's deadliest conflict zones.

Vinci Books

vinci-books.com

Published by Vinci Books Ltd in 2025

1

Copyright © Jack Silkstone 2016

A CIP catalogue record for this book is available from the British Library.

Paperback ISBN: 9781036703851

The EU GPSR authorised representative is Logos Europe, 9 rue Nicolas Poussion, 17000 La Rochelle, France
contact@logoseurope.eu

By Jack Silkstone

SEAL

SEAL of Approval
SEAL the Deal
Signed SEAL'd and Delivered

Chapter One

Special Warfare Operator Mike Saunders placed the two halves of his M4 carbine on his desk and glanced at the Belgian Malinois working dog that sat at his feet. Reaching down he ruffled the hound's ears and was rewarded with a snuffle from a wet nose. Smiling, he returned to cleaning his weapon and watching the video playing on his battered laptop.

Tall, with broad shoulders, Mike looked as if he had stepped out of a SEAL recruiting poster. The twenty-eight year old had a square jaw, slate gray eyes, and short blonde hair. A cheeky smile and an easygoing attitude topped off what most women called a 'complete package'.

His dog, Axe, was an equally handsome specimen. Smaller and leaner than the related German Shepherd, he had a dark face with intelligent brown eyes and alert ears that jutted from the top of his head. That is, except for the very tip of his right ear which drooped forward like a wilted leaf.

Mike finished cleaning a component and scanned the

SEAL team room. Richard 'Rick' Anderson and Javier 'Ernie' Ernesto were also working on their weapons in a space resembling a football locker room. The men, and Axe, were team-mates, SEALs on standby at their base in Coronado, ready to leap into action, at a moment's notice.

"Hey Mike, how's that lady of yours doing? She launched her modeling agency yet?" asked Rick, a muscular African American who was the squad Corpsman and a notorious ladies man.

Mike snorted. "The party's tomorrow. And before you ask, you're not invited."

"Bro, you're killing me. What's the point of knowing someone who owns an agency if you're not allowed to meet the girls?"

"Meet, is that what you call it?" added Ernie from the bench seat where he was cleaning his pistol. The short, athletic Mexican was the squad's communications guy, happily married, and a father of two.

Rick flexed his bicep against the fabric of his camouflage combat shirt. "Hey, it's not my problem ladies can't resist, the Rick."

Mike finished assembling his carbine. "Did you seriously just refer to yourself in the third person?"

"Rick Slade gets all the ladies."

"The only thing Rick Slade's going to get is herpes," quipped Ernie.

Mike snickered. "Burn!"

At that moment a craggy-faced, barrel-chested SEAL with short gray hair barged into the room and bellowed. "Grab your panties ladies. We've got a hit on Barbosa. Wheels up in ten."

Chief 'TJ' Lines was their squad leader. Mike guessed his age at mid-forties but no one actually knew how old he was. He'd been a SEAL for longer than anyone could remember.

The men sprang into action, fitting their weapons together and grabbing their gear. Camouflage body armor covered with pouches was thrown on over their fatigues along with backpacks and their night vision equipped helmets.

Mike snapped his gun belt around his waist and checked his pistol was secure. "Where's he at?"

"Location of interest on the outskirts of Puerto. We've got approval. The platoon's launching and we're on point. I'll give orders in the air."

"Nice, going after the top dog," said Rick as he grabbed his medical kit.

"Only way we roll," added Ernie as he finished donning his own gear and made for the door. "I'll see you boys in the hangar. I wanna grab some extra batteries."

"I'll come with." Rick followed the comms guy out of the team room, leaving Mike and TJ with Axe. Mike finished fitting the dog's harness then rechecked all the buckles were closed. As he snapped on a lead, his laptop started chiming. He glanced at the flashing icon on the screen.

His girlfriend, Stacey, was calling. He locked eyes with a frowning TJ. "It'll only take a minute."

"You've got thirty seconds." The Chief continued preparing his equipment.

As the call connected Mike looked down at Axe's intelligent eyes staring up at him. "Just a second, bud."

The call connected and an attractive blonde appeared on screen. "Michael, where are you?" Her high-pitched voice crackled through the speakers.

He fought the urge to grimace and braced himself as he

delivered the bad news. "At work babe, 'bout to head out the door."

Stacey's heavily made-up face screwed into a scowl. "What do you mean you're heading out? Where are you going?"

"Honey, I can't tell you. You know how it is."

One perfectly manicured eyebrow arched. "Really, you're going to play that card. You do realize that my agency launch is tomorrow?" She flicked her hair to emphasize the point.

"Of course, look I'm going to do my best to get there but—"

"But? All I ever hear are excuses, Michael. I'm beginning to think that you've got zero interest in this relationship."

"Hey, you know that's not true."

"Then make sure you're here tomorrow night." Her face disappeared as she terminated the call.

Mike glanced down and took in the concerned expression on Axe's dark face.

"Yeah, I know bro." He took up the dog's lead.

"Walk with me, Mike," grunted TJ from the doorway.

The three of them, two operators and a canine, left the SEAL's training facility in the direction of the Naval Air Station hangars.

"You might not know this, Mike, but when I first joined the teams, I was married." The old SEAL had a voice that sounded like gravel being tossed in a steel drum. "It didn't last very long. You know why?"

Mike could guess why. "No, tell me."

"Because she was a narcissistic princess. A lot like that pretty little lady you're fooling around with. Bud, SEALs and girls like that don't work... not long term."

At a loss for words, Mike remained silent.

"Yeah, they're fun and she's probably a great lay, but that's it. You can't count on them. They're about as reliable as a cheesecloth condom. Soon as things get tough, they're going to cause you heartache and headaches. Isn't that right, Axe?"

At the sound of his name, the dog glanced up at TJ and licked his chops.

"See, even Axe agrees."

They entered a cavernous aircraft hangar and joined the rest of the squad. Rick and Ernie had organized their parachute rigs and other equipment. Behind them, the rest of the SEAL platoon, another ten men, also prepared their gear.

"That lady of yours doesn't look or sound like the sort of woman a SEAL should be dating, brother," continued TJ as he found his rig in the line of parachutes.

Rick laughed as he adjusted his harness. "The old man giving another one of his infamous lectures?"

"Hey, I'm just trying to look out for our boy. That's what brothers do."

"I get it, TJ, and I appreciate your advice, but I think you're wrong about Stacey. She's a good person. She's just got a lot riding on this agency." Mike adjusted his own chute, checking the suspension hooks that would hold Axe across his chest.

Rick snorted. "She may be hot but, that woman's crazy with a capital C."

Mike frowned and turned to Ernie for support.

"Whoa, brother, don't bring me in on this." Ernie tossed Mike a *Starburst*, his favorite. "Who you choose to date is completely up to you." He lowered his eyes to his equipment. "But *essè*, the bitch is crazy. I mean, who the hell hacks their boyfriend's email account."

"She's a little insecure," said Mike as he unwrapped the candy.

"Bro, she chooses what you wear," added Rick. "And then, when you don't wear it she refuses to go out with you. That girl is all about herself."

Mike chewed the *Starburst* as he glanced down at Axe sitting at his feet. "What about you bud, you like Stacey, right?"

The dog gave a whine as he lowered himself to the floor and covered his snout with one paw as the others broke into laughter. Mike shook his head in disgust.

TJ gave him a friendly slap on the back. "Hey, like I said, bud. We're just looking out for our team-mate. Now, let's get this show on the road."

On the other side of town, at the Iron Canyon Veterinary Clinic, Alison Taylor was finishing her final consult for the day. Chloe, a beautiful Golden Retriever sat on her examination table. It had been a last minute walk-in to the clinic. Chloe had chased a squirrel over an embankment and badly sprained her hind leg. Faced with an injured dog and a distressed owner, Alison had been unable to turn them away.

With the dog bandaged and her owner placated, the pretty veterinarian glanced at the clock on the wall, as she washed her hands.

"Oh crap!" It was already ten past seven. She was late for her date.

She slipped out of her scrubs and fished a flowery

summer dress from a sports bag in the corner of her office. Throwing on a pair of black flats with the dress she turned and faced the mirror on the back of the door. She grimaced. The face looking back at her might have been pretty, if it wasn't for the bags under her eyes. She pulled her long brown hair into a ponytail, applied color to her full lips, traced liner around her green eyes and dusted her cheeks with a touch of concealer. She was far from ready. But, it would have to do.

Her assistant caught her on the way out. "Have a good time."

The restaurant was a short cab ride from the clinic. On the way, she checked her phone. She had three missed calls from Brian, her date. The banker would not be impressed by her tardiness.

A smartly dressed maître d' led her to the table where Brian was waiting. The handsome investment banker was dressed in a three-piece suit and wore a frown. She noted he already had a starter in front of him and a glass of wine.

She felt his gaze on her as she approached.

Smiling, she reached the table. "So sorry I'm late. I had a last minute consult."

Brian remained seated. "I took the liberty of ordering you the salad."

The waiter pulled her chair out and Alison sat. "Oh… thank you."

The banker frowned. "I hope that's alright. I mean this is a two star restaurant and I didn't want to offend them by not ordering."

Alison managed a thin smile. "No, it's fine. A salad is perfect. I can always get the steak for entrée."

"I did tell you it was a two star restaurant didn't I?"

"A number of times, why? Is there a problem?"

7

He exhaled. "It's just... Look, the owner is a client of my firm and..."

Alison's face suddenly felt warm. "Go on."

He leaned forward and whispered. "And, well you didn't put very much effort into your presentation."

It took every ounce of her strength to refrain from taking his glass of wine and throwing it in his face. Instead she whispered back. "Like I said, I had a last minute consult."

He chuckled. "Please, I'm sure the dog's sprained ankle could have waited."

She grabbed her glass of water and drank to hide her disgust.

"Look, it's OK," he continued. "Just, for future reference, it's appropriate to wear heels to a restaurant like this."

The waiter appeared with a bottle of wine and Brian inspected it. "So, I had quite the hectic day today."

Alison didn't hear the rest of the words coming from his mouth. Her mind had wandered back to their first date. A casual drink at a bar, it had gone reasonably well. In direct contrast to his current behavior, Brian had been attentive, engaging and somewhat charming.

"Alison!"

She turned her attention back to him.

"Did you hear anything I said?"

She shook her head. "I'm sorry. Look, I'm not feeling very well. I might slip out to the ladies room. I'll also fix up my makeup."

He nodded. "Good idea."

"Excuse me." She rose from the table and made her way to the foyer. Instead of entering the restrooms, she ducked out of the restaurant and hailed a cab. Climbing in, she slumped into the back seat and fought back tears.

The driver glanced at her in the mirror. "Where to, Miss?"

She gave him her address and reached into her bag for her phone. The number she wanted was at the top of her favorites.

Her sister Leonie, answered. "Hey sis, I thought you were on a hot date."

"Things didn't turn out the way I expected."

"Are you OK? What happened?"

Alison gave her a run down on the brief encounter with Brian.

"You're kidding me? He actually said that? What an A-grade asshole."

"Yeah, I'm beginning to think I attract them."

"No babe, there's just a lot of them in the world. Look, where are you now?"

"On my way home."

"Screw that. Meet me at the *Cold Stone* at Rancho Del Ray. Triple choc ice cream will make you feel better."

Alison managed a chuckle. "Fine, but I'm telling you now. I'm done with men and I'm done with dating."

"Good, ice cream it is."

Mike rested a gloved hand on Axe's head and ruffled his ears. He could feel the animal's excitement; a bundle of barely contained energy pressed against his leg. The two of them, and the three other members of the squad, were hidden in a tree line a few hundred feet from the walls of a gated hacienda. If their intelligence was correct, and it so often wasn't, then one of the most wanted men in Mexico currently resided inside the lavish mansion.

9

Vicente Barbosa, or as his men called him, Barbosa the Butcher, was a Sinaloa Cartel kingpin responsible for the death of hundreds, possibly thousands, of Mexicans. However, that wasn't why he'd made it onto the target deck of the SEALs. It was for a far more personal reason as far as the United States Government was concerned.

Six months earlier, the CIA had linked him to the abduction and murder of a US citizen, a teenage girl. She also happened to be the niece of a high-ranking American Diplomat. With that act Barbosa earned himself the undivided attention of Predator drones, surveillance satellites, and teams of analysts at both the CIA and NSA. An elusive target at the best of times, the outcry over the murder had driven him underground. Finally, they had isolated his location to this multi-story, walled estate deep within Sinaloa Cartel territory. And now, justice was going to be served.

Mike had parachuted, along with the rest of his platoon, from a C-130 transport aircraft with Axe strapped to his chest. It was the veteran working dog's tenth operational jump and it had gone off without a hitch. Highly trained, Axe was a vital component of the squad and couldn't be left behind. His sensitive nose detected hidden booby traps, tracked fleeing targets, and with his razor-sharp teeth he could dissuade most bad guys from putting up a fight.

From the darkness, he heard Rick's whisper. "How long till we get this rock show on the road?"

Mike turned his head so he could see the Corpsman through his night vision goggles.

"We keeping you from a hot date, gunslinger?" growled TJ from behind them.

"Nah, we're just giving the Butcher plenty of time to slip away."

Ernie lifted his head from the glowing radio panel.

"Some of the other squads are having problems getting into position. The scrub around the back is pretty thick. Going to be at least another twenty."

"Always waiting," mumbled Rick, leaning back against his medical pack with his weapon held across his knees.

Mike gave Axe a reassuring pat, turned back to their target and scanned the walls of the hacienda. At least ten feet high, they posed a significant obstacle. Fortunately, the solid metal gates that guarded the entrance were wide open.

"Ghost One is reporting no significant activity on the target," whispered Ernie.

Ghost was the call sign of the Predator drone that was watching the compound from above.

"Yay, Intel probably fucked up again," said Rick.

"Regular ray of goddamn sunshine tonight, aren't you?" said TJ.

Rick snorted. "Well, I've got nothing to look forward to now, do I Mike? Stacey's party was going to be the highlight of my month."

Mike sighed. He'd managed to suppress all thoughts of Stacey and her threats, but now she was back on his mind. It had been almost six months since he'd met her in a bar in town. Vibrant, bright and sexy, the chemistry between them had been explosive. Now, he was forced to admit their relationship was almost purely physical. Yes it was fun. Hell, it was intense. But, once out of the bedroom the lack of connection left him empty. Worse still, TJ's assessment was spot on. She wasn't a team player and that wasn't going to change anytime soon.

"Ghost One's spotted movement." Ernie's voice snapped him back to the task at hand.

"Are the cut-off teams in place?" asked TJ.

"Negative, Ghost has eyes on five people gathering around a vehicle in front of the hacienda."

"The Butcher's about to leave the building," hissed Rick.

"The boss wants us to roll now," added Ernie.

"Roger. Mike, you and Axe are on point," ordered TJ. "We'll take down the targets at the car and then move inside."

Mike unsnapped the lead from Axe's harness, releasing him. He felt the dog tense with excitement. "Axe, wait." Gripping his carbine tightly, he waited for TJ to tap him on the shoulder.

———

As Mike moved through the front gates of the hacienda, he spotted a group of men clustered around a black SUV. The car's doors were open.

"Hands up, hands up!" TJ bellowed.

The men went for their weapons and Mike fired. His carbine bucked against his shoulder as his target dropped. Why did they always try to fight, he thought as he engaged another gunman. "Axe, down," he ordered as an AK blasted. The dog dropped to his belly.

Ernie and Rick made short work of the other cartel thugs. Then, as a team, they moved forward and checked the bodies.

"Vehicle's empty. Butcher must be inside," said TJ.

With the Chief off his shoulder and Axe by his side, Mike crept up the stairs. "OK boy, search."

The dog wagged his tail. Trained to locate, and if necessary, neutralize any potential threats, he trotted forward.

Weapon held ready Mike followed him into the foyer.

Axe ignored the staircase that led to the second level and stopped in front of a heavy wooden door. Halting beside his partner Mike scanned the ornate fixtures and whispered, "Guy sure likes to throw some cash around."

"Perks of the business." TJ leaned across and checked the door handle. As it turned a gun fired. Bullets punched through the wood next to his face. "We've got a live one."

As Rick and Ernie joined them in the foyer Mike returned fire. "Need a breach!"

"Heads up." Rick tossed him an explosive charge.

He caught it and stuck it to the door. "Take cover." He yanked the initiator. As the fuse spluttered he pulled Axe back and placed his gloved hands over the dog's ears.

The explosive charge detonated with a loud bang. The doors flew open with a blast of smoke and debris.

"Axe, hunt." The dog dashed into the room, closely followed by TJ. Readying his weapon, Mike charged into the room on their heels.

TJ's suppressed weapon snapped. An armed gunman took a bullet to the face. Mike spotted another man behind a desk. The Butcher. His pistol was aimed at them. His head filled Mike's sights.

A flash of fur and teeth flew through the air. Axe clamped onto the cartel boss's arm, dragging him to the ground. The Butcher screamed as the dog bit down, hard.

TJ was the first to reach him. He jabbed the suppressor of his carbine in his face and yelled, "Shut the fuck up!"

Mike kicked the pistol clear. "Axe, release."

"Roll over. Face down," ordered TJ.

Reluctantly, the overweight Mexican rolled onto his front. Every time he lifted his head Axe snarled, savagely.

"Keep that beast away from me," whimpered the Butcher.

Mike checked the Mexican's arm as he cuffed him. Axe had left puncture marks but hadn't drawn blood. "Shut up or I'll let him eat it."

Ernie stuck his head into the office. "TJ, we've got a problem. Bravo squad has spotted two vehicles inbound on our position."

"They didn't intercept?"

"Negative, they're still short of the cut-off location."

"Shit, what about Charlie?"

"They're moving to our location now, ETA five minutes."

The Butcher laughed. "You've bitten off more than you can chew *culero*, my people are going to kill you all."

"Axe, guard."

A low rumbling growl silenced the Mexican.

TJ removed his helmet and rubbed his scalp. "ETA of the vehicles?"

"Under a minute."

"I say we hit 'em from the front door and hold them off till Charlie gets here," suggested Rick.

"Axe can guard the Butcher," added Mike.

"Let's do it." TJ fastened his helmet as he dashed back out into the foyer. He knelt a few feet from the open doorway and aimed his weapon at the front gate.

Ernie and Rick followed suit. The Corpsman smashed out one of the tall windows that framed the doorway so he could fire through it.

"Axe, guard." Mike poked the corpulent cartel boss with the toe of his boot. "I wouldn't move if I were you. He'll tear out your throat."

The dog gave a blood-curdling growl as if to emphasize the point.

Joining the others, Mike swapped out the magazine on

his carbine. They'd killed the lights to hide from the approaching vehicles.

Ten long seconds later a black Chevy SUV roared through the front gates, skidding to a stop on the manicured lawn. The SEALs hit it with a devastating fusillade of fire. Windows shattered as their bullets shredded most of the occupants.

At least two men managed to escape. They returned fire as the second SUV shuddered to a halt behind the first. Mike switched his aim and pumped a half dozen rounds into it. His bullets skipped off the glass without penetrating. "Number two is armored."

An AK barked and bullets hit the doorway forcing TJ back as men spilled from the new vehicle.

"Fall back!" TJ yelled.

Ernie went first, followed by Rick. The pair took up positions at the door to a study, allowing TJ and Mike to move back to where Axe guarded the Butcher.

"Where the hell is Charlie?" screamed Rick as he covered them from the doorway.

Bullets smacked into the hacienda as the men outside unleashed everything they had on the SEALs.

"They're close, real close." Ernie wrenched open a door at the back of the study. "We can get out here."

"Grab the Butcher," said TJ.

Mike hauled the Mexican off the floor. "Axe, with me."

A volley of bullets shattered one of the office's windows. The Butcher broke free of Mike and dove through the opening.

"Oh shit." Mike hurtled through the window after him. As he crashed onto the gravel footpath, his weapon was flung clear and the Butcher sprinted away.

Stumbling to his feet, Mike spotted two men headed

toward him, guns raised. Snatching up his carbine, he fired, hitting one of them. Time slowed as he realized that the second man had the drop on him. He looked directly into the gaping black muzzle of the man's pistol while he tried to bring his weapon to bear.

A flash of brown fur leaped from the hacienda. Axe hit the gunman, his jaws snapping closed on his arm as they collapsed to the ground. The pistol roared. Axe yelped.

Struggling to his feet, the shooter pushed the dog clear. As he raised his pistol to finish Axe, Mike fired. The carbine bucked in his shoulder. The gunman toppled over, dead.

Oblivious to Charlie squad's arrival, and elimination of the remaining gunmen, Mike sprinted to Axe's side and focused on the gaping gunshot wound in his partner's hindquarter. Tearing a field dressing from his pouch, he pressed the pad against the bloody hole. "Stay with me Axe. Stay with me boy."

The dog looked up at him with trusting eyes.

Mike struggled to control his emotions as he fought to stem the flow of blood.

Rick knelt next to him and dropped his medical kit to the ground. "Keep the pressure on." He pulled a razor-sharp knife from his vest and shaved a patch of fur off the Axe's front leg. He injected a painkiller and inserted an IV line in the exposed vein. Handing the bag of fluid to Mike, Rick inspected the wound. "OK, we're going to need to plug both sides before we can move him. "Ernie, what's our ETA on the chopper?"

"Ten minutes out. How's he doing?" the comms guy replied.

Rick nodded and dove back into his medical kit for another bandage.

As Mike stroked Axe's muzzle he noted the dog's eyes

were glassy from the combined painkiller and blood loss. He ignored the SEALs from Charlie as they ran past to secure the perimeter. The beat of an approaching helicopter's rotors barely registered. It wasn't till Axe was in the hands of a USAF MEDEVAC team and the SEALs were extracting that Mike turned to TJ. "What happened to the Butcher?"

"He got away."

"Damn it, I messed up."

The Chief grasped his shoulder. "Not at all, bud. The guy who shot Axe, the one you slotted, that was Juan Barbosa, the Butcher's brother and right hand man. You and Axe took down a high value target."

"Yeah, let's hope Axe makes it." Mike wiped his eyes with his sleeve.

"He's a goddamn frog dog brother, he'll make it."

Chapter Two

The sun had barely crept above the horizon as Mike watched the USAF medical staff unload Axe from the C-130 cargo plane. The dog had been unconscious since Rick had sedated him and Mike had not left his side.

He handed his weapons and ammunition to TJ, before joining the dog in an ambulance. It was a short ride from Coronado to the veterinary facility at Marine Corps Air Station Miramar. Upon arrival, the staff were ready and waiting.

A nurse dressed in green scrubs blocked Mike from following the stretcher into the operating room "Sir, you can't go any further than this. You'll have to wait out here." She must have read the grief on his face as she added. "I'll have one of the girls get you a coffee. And as soon as he's stable I'll bring you in, OK?"

Mike nodded and collapsed into a seat in the waiting room. He sat quietly for a moment. Then it hit him, he was still wearing his body armor and helmet. Stripping off the items, he dumped them onto the seat next to him.

A young civilian receptionist offered him a cup of hot coffee.

"Do you need anything else?" she asked softly.

He shook his head and accepted the coffee gratefully.

"They're going to be in surgery for a few hours. So, you might want to duck away, grab a shower and a change clothes."

Mike glanced down at his uniform; it was covered in dried blood, Axe's blood. "No, I'm staying here till he's out."

She smiled, gave him a knowing nod and returned to behind the counter.

Finishing the coffee, he leaned back, trying to get comfortable in the hard plastic chair. He glanced up at the wall clock and noted the time. It was five after seven in the morning. Twenty minutes, he'd only been in the surgery for twenty minutes. It felt like Axe had been in there for hours.

Exhaling, he closed his eyes and tipped his head back against the wall. He really should give Stacey a call and let her know he was back. No, he couldn't deal with her right now. He hadn't slept in over twenty-four hours and she would be focused on her launch.

A gentle nudge woke Mike. His eyes snapped open and he jolted upright.

"Hey, brother," said TJ.

He checked the clock. Shit, it was nearly ten. Somehow, despite the stress he'd managed almost three hours of sleep. Spotting Rick at the counter talking to the receptionist, he leaped out of his seat. "Is he out of surgery?"

Rick turned to face him. "Not yet, bud."

"It shouldn't be much longer," added the receptionist.

The door to the waiting room opened and Ernie joined the rest of the squad. He handed Mike his cell phone and a takeout box. "Thought you might want some breakfast. Any news?"

Mike forced a smile as he took the items and resumed his seat. "Thanks, no news yet, he's still in surgery." He checked his phone; thirteen missed calls, all from Stacey. Before he could call her back, the smell of the food in the box hit him and his stomach growled. He hadn't realized he was starving. Opening the container revealed a breakfast burrito. Stacey had waited this long, what was a few more minutes.

As Mike devoured the spicy Mexican food, Ernie grinned. "Maria dropped them round."

"That woman is an angel," added TJ as he took a seat.

"An angel who gave birth to devil spawn," grunted Ernie as he took the chair opposite Mike. "You know what they did last night?"

"No, what?" he asked before taking another bite.

"They cut the TV power cord and set the sofa on fire."

TJ frowned. "They OK?"

"Of course. They're the spawn of Satan. So, yeah, they're fine."

TJ winked. "I think that might be the influence of their father."

Mike wiped his chin. "Hey, thanks for coming down guys."

"Bro, Axe is our team-mate too," Rick said, abandoning his pursuit of the receptionist and taking a seat facing Mike.

As he tossed the empty box in the trash his phone started ringing. He glanced at the screen. It was Stacey. He answered it. "Hey babe, look–"

"Don't 'hey babe' me. Where the hell are you?"

"At the base. Axe has been–"

"You're at the base! Have you forgotten this is the most important day of my life?" she shrieked.

Grimacing, Mike angled the speaker away from his ear. "Babe, babe, listen to me."

"No, you listen to me, Michael Saunders. You get yourself over here now or we're finished."

"Stacey, please. Axe has been shot, he's in surgery."

There was a pause. "Michael, he's a dog. This agency is my future. And what I'm hearing is that you think a dog is more important than my future?"

Sighing, Mike placed a clenched fist against his forehead. "I can't leave until I know he's going to be OK."

"Then you and I are done."

"Stacey, don't be like that... Stacey?" Mike checked the phone. She had terminated the call. He glanced at his team members. All of them were looking away, pretending not to have listened. "She just broke up with me."

Before anyone could respond a man strode into the room wearing bloodied scrubs.

Mike dropped the phone to his side and rose. "Is he going to be OK?"

The veterinarian nodded. "The short answer is he'll live."

"And the long answer?" asked TJ.

"I'm not sure if he'll ever walk properly again."

Rick leaned forward. "But, he's out of danger?"

"Yes, he's waking now."

Mike fought back tears. "Can I see him?"

The vet glanced at TJ who wore a stern expression. "Yes, but only for a moment. He needs to rest."

Mike followed the vet through to the recovery room. Axe lay in a wide cage with the door open. His rear leg had been shaved. The angry red wound had been stapled shut.

When the dog saw him his ears rose and he attempted to sit.

"Axe, down, stay." Mike squatted and patted the dog. A tear ran down his cheek as he ruffled the ears. "I thought I'd lost you boy."

Axe lifted his head and licked Mike's hand. Then he lowered his head and closed his eyes.

"He's lost a lot of blood and needs to rest," said the vet.

Mike kissed the dog's head. "I'll come back soon." Blinking hard he gave him one last pat before returning to the waiting room and the concerned expressions of the rest of his team.

"All things considered… he looks good," said Mike as he reached for his phone.

TJ clasped his shoulder. "Who ya calling, slick?"

"Stacey. If I rush, I can still help her set up for the function."

"Nope. Not happening." TJ snatched the phone from his hand. "You're heading back to the team room for a shower. Afterward, we're running through a debrief. You can have your phone back when we're done."

Lacking the energy to argue, Mike followed the team out to the parking lot. Spotting Ernie's SUV, he climbed in the back. TJ was right. The op had been a cluster fuck, a debrief might provide insight as to why.

Hot water streamed over Mike's head and down his aching back. Bracing against the wall he let the warmth soak into every muscle. Finally cleansed of the grime and fatigue of the last twenty-four hours, he dried himself, dressed in shorts and a T-shirt, and joined the others in the team room. "We gonna do this debriefing or what?"

TJ lifted a cooler onto a bench seat and opened it. He pulled out a can of *Coors* and handed it to Mike. "Debrief can wait. We need to lift a beer for Axe."

He offered one to Rick, but the Corpsman waved it away. Instead, he opened his locker and rummaged inside. "If we're raising a drink for Axe it should be something a little stiffer." He revealed a bottle of *Pyrat Rum* and four empty 40 mm grenade casings. "Our boy deserves the best yeah?" He placed them on the bench next to the cooler.

Mike nodded. "The best for the best. Although, I'm going to chase that with one of TJ's beers."

Ernie added a bottle of *Gran Dovejo Reposado Tequila* to the mix. "Not before you have a shot of this."

"I didn't realize I was rolling with a squad of alcoholics," TJ said as he splashed rum into each of the metal casings and all four men lifted them toward the ceiling.

"For Axe, the best sidekick a SEAL could have," said Mike.

"A goddamn frog dog through and through," added TJ.

"Axe!" they echoed.

They downed their shots, then Mike took a swig from his beer as TJ refilled the casings with a healthy slug of tequila.

"I've got a toast," said Rick.

"Fire away," said TJ.

"To Mike and his freedom. Welcome back to single life, brother."

Mike frowned as he downed the tequila shot. "TJ, I need my phone back. I've got to call Stacey."

The grizzled Chief shook his head. "You don't wanna do that, bud. She's not right for you."

Mike contemplated the statement as the alcohol warmed his stomach. "I guess not. I mean, she dumped me because I couldn't make her launch party."

Rick sloshed more rum into his 40 mm casing. "Dude, your partner got shot. It's not like you didn't want to be there. You tried your best, brother."

TJ nodded. "Any woman who dates a SEAL needs to know, when you're on the job, the team comes first. Women like her… self-absorbed 'n' all. She's never going to understand honor, courage and commitment."

Mike took a sip and savored the burn as it slid down his throat. "Yeah, you know, she's kind of selfish, right?"

The other men laughed as they drank.

"Good looking," said Rick, "but a total bitch."

"Total bitch," echoed Ernie.

"You know boys," TJ added reflectively.

"Helmets on." Rick chuckled. "Here comes another war story."

"Shut the hell up, Rick. This is important." The Chief took another swig from his beer. "You know what the problem with women is?"

"They nag you about everything?" said Ernie.

TJ scowled. "Your wife's an angel, Ernie. Most men aren't that lucky."

"I'll drink to that." Rick charged their 40 mm casings with rum. "My ex-wife was a goddamn nightmare. Whereas, your wife, Ernie, is patient, dedicated, smart, an awesome mother and she's beautiful. She's way too good for you."

The men all toasted Ernie's wife, Maria.

Mike reached for his beer and chased the rum with a healthy swig. He was starting to feel the effect of the booze.

Aches and bruises were forgotten along with Stacey. "TJ, what were you saying?"

The Chief squinted in thought. "Oh yeah, I was going to explain the difference between SEALs and women." He finished his beer and cracked a new one. "Rick, why is it that when a newbie joins the squad you know you can trust him?"

"That's easy, bro. It's because he's been through BUD and SQT. He's a goddamn frogman."

"That's right. He's been selected for the right attributes, trained in the basic skills, put through the wringer and as a result you know he's good to go."

Mike snorted beer from his nose. "TJ, are you saying what I think you're saying?"

"Damn straight. If you want to make sure you've got a good woman, you've got to run her through a selection process, just like BUD."

Rick laughed. "I don't wanna date a woman who can pass that shit, bro. Did you see Demi Moore in G.I. Jane? That chick had bigger guns than Mike."

"Hey, come on. Mike's are pretty massive." Ernie chuckled as he poured another round of tequila.

"Not BUD, you thick sons of bitches," TJ continued. "A selection process especially for women. One that reveals who they really are, a woman, no, a girlfriend selection course. That's it, a Girlfriend Selection Course."

Rick nodded as he downed another shot. "Golf, Sierra, Charlie. I love it. We test Mike's next girlfriend to make sure she's not a narcissistic, princess, cow."

"Hey, what about you?" said Mike.

"Bud, I love narcissistic, princess, cows. I'm just not about to marry another one. You're the dude who falls for princesses and wears his heart on his sleeve. Hell, you're a walk over boy. Girls have you eating out of their hands on the second date. You're a goddamn dream boat."

Ernie nodded in agreement. "It's true, *essé*."

"So that's that." TJ lifted his 40 mm casing. "The next time Mike gets serious, we're gonna run a selection course. Boom!"

Mike frowned. "Guys, I'm not sure about this."

TJ sloshed more rum into his casing. "Brother, this is for your own good."

Chapter Three

Head aching Mike pushed the vet's door open and strode to the counter. Lifting his sunglasses, he shot the receptionist a weary smile. "Hi, I'm here to see Axe."

As she opened her mouth to respond, he heard a loud bark from behind her. "That would be him now," she managed as the aggressive barking continued.

Hangover forgotten, Mike pushed open the door to the recovery area, entered the room and stood dead in his tracks at the sight before him. The Army veterinarian was perched on a steel examination table. Axe had made it half way out of his cage, barking with his hind legs dragging behind him.

Mike approached slowly. "Hey, easy boy, easy."

Axe's demeanor changed instantly. His ears rose and he stopped barking. Instead he tried to scrabble across the floor to Mike.

"Axe, stay!" He knelt and lifted the dog back into the cage. Axe gave a soft whimper and licked his face. Mike did his best to make the dog comfortable, stroking his muzzle as he adjusted the bedding. "Hey, it's OK, buddy. I'm here, everything's going to be fine."

The vet climbed off the table and hid behind Mike. "He wouldn't let me check the wound. Went crazy as soon as I touched him."

"I think he's a little stressed from the incident. He should be fine now I'm here."

The vet squatted alongside him and reached in to check the bandages around the dog's hind leg.

Axe gave a low growl and bared his teeth.

"Axe, no!"

The vet backed off, raising his hands in the air. "I give up. I can't get close to him. You're going to have to change his bandages."

"No problem." Trained in combat first aid, Mike didn't have any difficulties inspecting the wounds. He checked the flesh around the surgical staples for tenderness and infection, there was none. The vet handed him fresh bandages and he changed the pad covering the wound. Then he sat with the dog, ruffling his ears. Axe's eyes never left the vet. "What's the prognosis, doc?"

The vet leaned against the stainless-steel table watching Axe warily. "The bullet missed the bone but it destroyed a lot of muscle and ligaments. I'm not sure how it'll heal. Then there's his attitude. If I can't get close to him I can't treat him."

"I can come in every day."

"That would help."

Axe nuzzled Mike's hand prompting him for another pat. The dog sighed, relaxing, and finally took his eyes off the vet.

"Do you think he'll work again?"

The vet shook his head. "No, his days of chasing down bad guys are over."

Mike continued to stroke the dog's ears. "You hear that, boy. Looks like it's going to be all ball-chasing and lying in the sun from here on." In spite of his words, Mike felt empty. The idea of going to work each day, and not having Axe by his side, would take time to come to terms with.

Remembering work, he checked his watch. Crap, he was going to be late. He gave Axe another pat. "I've got to get going, buddy, be good for the doc."

"That would make a nice change," said the vet.

Mike closed the dog's cage. As he rose Axe whined while glancing up at him with sad brown eyes. "Hey, none of that. I'll be back this afternoon." Mike gave him one last pat through the mesh and followed the vet out into the waiting area.

"He's a good dog, Mike. But, if we can't turn his temperament around we're going to have problems."

Mike shook his hand. "He'll be fine." Then he ducked out of the door to his pickup. As he drove across town to Coronado, he couldn't help but worry that Axe's attitude change might be permanent.

Mike pulled up to the twenty-five yard shooting range and joined the rest of his squad for training.

He spotted TJ at the ammunition point, loading magazines from a box of cartridges. The Chief looked fresh despite a heavy night's drinking.

"Hey bud, how's Axe?"

"He's OK, the wound looks like it'll heal." He found his weapons in the squad trunk and laid them on the ground before joining TJ to fill magazines.

Already at the firing point, the other squad members were shooting their suppressed carbines at paper targets.

Mike and TJ worked in silence for a few minutes before TJ spoke again. "You wanna tell me what's eating at you?"

Mike dropped a half-filled magazine on the bench. "He won't let the vet near him. I've never seen him like this, TJ, his entire temperament has changed."

"Bud, I've seen the same thing in operators. They take a big hit like that and suddenly they're jumping at shadows and snapping at their closest friends. Sounds like your boy's got post-traumatic stress disorder. When are they going to let you bring him back to work?"

"They're not. Vet says he's done."

"Shit bud." TJ reached out and grasped his shoulder. "I'm sorry, he was a great working dog."

"Hey, what's up?" asked Rick as he and Ernie joined them.

"Axe is going to be retired," said Mike.

"Ah crap. I'm sorry, dude," said Ernie.

"That's shit bro, he's an amazing dog," added Rick.

Mike sighed. "The big problem isn't his leg. He won't let anyone near him, except me. TJ thinks he might have PTSD."

Rick nodded. "Yeah that makes sense. Getting shot messes with the best of us. But he'll be OK in the long run. You'll keep him, right?"

"How can I? We're out on jobs every second day and I can't leave him with just anyone."

"I'd take him," added Ernie. "But with the kids…"

"I understand," said Mike.

"Look, if you need to take some time off I can talk to the Skipper," said TJ.

"Yeah, I might have to." Mike picked up his magazine and went back to loading it. The others did likewise.

"Ernie, that little rat dog your mother has," said Rick. "I remember it being a total shit head. Who sorted it out, when her neighbor's mutt tried to eat it?"

Ernie scowled. "That 'rat' was a pedigree Chihuahua, you idiot. Yeah, someone did help her. My brother found a vet out near Iron Canyon who specializes in traumatized dogs."

"And she fixed your Mom's Chihuahua?" asked Mike.

Ernie nodded. "Allegedly, she's Dr. Doolittle or something."

Mike managed a laugh. "I think Axe needs something a little heavier duty than a Chihuahua whisperer."

Ernie shrugged. "Maybe, my brother said she's real pretty."

It was Rick's turn to frown. "What the hell, bro? You never told me about a pretty vet."

"She's not your type."

"Not hot enough?"

"Too smart."

Laughing, the team moved down to the firing point. For the first time today, Mike managed a smile. It felt good to be surrounded by friends. Finding a spare target, he racked the action on his carbine and readied himself. Then, as he was about to squeeze off a round, his phone rang. Fearing the worst, he pulled it from his pocket and answered.

"So, you're finally going to answer my calls, Michael," snapped an angry voice.

Stacey, he mouthed to TJ. "Hey, look I'm—"

"I don't care!" she screamed.

Wincing, Mike held the phone at arm's length as she continued to rant. Suddenly, a gloved hand plucked it from his grasp.

"Standby!" TJ held it in the air. Stacey's voice still screeched from the speaker.

"Ready!" echoed Rick and Ernie, their weapons held tight.

"Up!"

The phone arced high in the air. Rick and Ernie's weapons spat suppressed rounds as they tracked it. Mike flinched as his smartphone disintegrated in a hail of lead.

"Nice shooting boys," said TJ. He turned to Mike and winked. "You need to change your number."

A few hours later Mike and the others were back in the team room when there was a knock at the door.

"Come in," bellowed TJ.

One of the headquarters' administration staff stuck his head inside.

"Hey Mack, what's up?"

The sailor gave TJ a nod. "The old man wants to see Mike in his office."

Mike frowned. "Just me?" It was rare for the commander to request the presence of an individual SEAL without their platoon chief.

"Yes."

"I'll get into a clean uniform."

"No need, boss just wants a chat," said the sailor. "I tried to call you but your number's disconnected."

Mike scowled at TJ. "Yeah, my phone's shot. I've got to get a new one."

Five minutes later, Mike waited outside Commander Conner's office. As he waited, he wondered why the 'old man' wanted to talk to him. The last time he'd spoken face-to-face with Team Five's C.O. was when he'd marched into the unit three years earlier. The thirty-five-year-old commander was a busy man, who rarely had the opportunity to spend individual time with the hundred-odd operators in his SEAL Team.

The door opened and the C.O. appeared. "Mike, come in and take a seat."

He stepped into the spacious office and sat in the chair opposite the commander. In the few seconds it took Conner to return to his desk Mike scanned the room. The walls were adorned with a handful of framed photos and plaques, but there were fewer than he expected for a ranking officer. In the corner, on a wooden stand, hung the commander's combat vest and helmet.

"Mike, I wanted to personally break this news to you. I know how important Axe is to you and your squad." He frowned as he pushed a piece of paper across his desk. "The veterinarian has submitted his report. The Navy has chosen to discharge Axe."

Mike nodded as he scanned the document. The information wasn't surprising. Axe was incapable of working and the Navy had no use for a Military Working Dog that couldn't work.

"There's more."

Mike glanced up. The commander continued, "Mike, the Navy is going to have him put down."

The words hit like a punch to the chest. "What? Boss,

they can't do that. He saved my life. Axe is a goddamn hero."

Conner exhaled. "I know Mike, but it's out of my control. The Navy can't risk retiring a dog that may attack someone. The vet submitted his report and the decision was made well above my pay grade. I tried to convince them otherwise, but they won't be swayed."

Mike swallowed hard. He wasn't about to shed a tear in front of his commanding officer. If the Navy had decided his dog's fate, there was nothing the C.O. could do.

"If you need any time off, Chief Lines will look after it. I've already spoken to him."

Mike nodded grimly.

"Son, as far as I am concerned that dog and you are both heroes. I wish there was more I could do."

Mike left the commander's office fighting the urge to punch the walls and scream with rage. Instead, he decided to confront the vet who had condemned his best friend to death. If he could convince him he wasn't dangerous, then maybe he could have the order revoked.

"Where you going, bud?" TJ's gravelly voice caught him by surprise.

Glancing left he spotted the Chief, Rick and Ernie waiting for him.

"They're going to kill Axe," said Mike.

TJ nodded. "We know."

Mike noticed the men were carrying black equipment bags. "What's going on?"

Ernie gave his bag a pat. "We grabbed some gear for tonight's job."

"What job?"

TJ wrapped an arm around his shoulder. "Operation Lumberjack. We're going to recover the Axe."

"We never leave a man behind, brother," added Rick. "Compared to hunting cartel douche bags this'll be a walk in the park."

"You do know he's being held on a Marine base?"

TJ chuckled. "Goddamn Taliban, Al-Qaida, Sinaloa, and Libyan bastards couldn't stop me. What makes you think a pack of Jarheads are gonna do any better?"

Chapter Four

Car headlights swept the parking lot of the veterinary facility. A vehicle pulled into a driveway on the opposite side of the street. It was three in the morning; late for a serviceman to be out on a Tuesday night.

Drunken singing carried on the night air. The driver helped her rather intoxicated Marine from the car up to the front door and they disappeared inside. A moment later the first-floor lights came on.

Mike's radio crackled as Ernie reported in. "Drunk leatherneck is home. We're all clear."

"OK Rick, let's do this," whispered Mike from where they hid in the trees at the edge of the parking lot. A dozen feet away Ernie lay in a thicket, where he kept watch on the road to the clinic. TJ waited in a minivan, parked up the road ready to make the pickup.

Rick led as they strolled casually from the trees, across the parking lot to the front door of the facility. Mike removed a lock-pick kit from his backpack. After inspecting the door, he chose the appropriate tool. Then, as he made to insert it, Rick slid a key into the lock.

"Where the hell did you get that?"

Rick flashed one of his signature smiles. "From Veronica." He pushed open the door and they slipped inside.

"Who the hell's Veronica?" asked Mike as an alarm gave a warning beep. He spotted the panel and made his way toward it.

"You know. The receptionist."

Mike stopped in his tracks. "You've been seeing the vet nurse? Bud, you talked to her for like three minutes."

He strolled nonchalantly across to the security panel and punched in a code. "Hey, what can I say? Ladies love the Rick."

The beeping stopped.

"She gave you the code?"

"Yeah, once I let her know how heartbroken you are about Axe. Told her you were weeping like a little girl. You should have seen it. Heart melted in about five seconds flat."

"Does TJ know about this?"

"Of course he does. Gramps knows everything. Now let's find that crazy mutt of yours and get the hell out of here."

Mike held up his hand. "Wait, so what happens when Axe is discovered missing and there's no sign of a break-in?"

Rick winked. "I've got a plan for that."

They crept through the foyer, down a short corridor into the recovery room. Mike eased the door open. "Axe, it's me buddy." Using a flashlight he located the cage and opened it. The dog gave a single excited bark.

Rick gave Axe a pat. "Hey bro."

Mike scooped the dog out of the cage and cradled him against his chest as he would a child. "Right, let's get out of here."

As they made their way back to the front door Rick contacted TJ on the radio. "We're ready for pickup, Pops."

The radio crackled. "You're ready for a punch in the face."

Rick laughed as they paused at the door and waited for the minivan to pull in to the parking lot. Once it stopped at the entrance he slid open the door and they loaded Axe inside.

Mike waited as Rick reactivated the alarm and locked the front door. Then TJ passed a wrench through the driver's window. Rick used it to smash one of the windows. As he leaped into the van a siren wailed.

"That's your plan?" Mike asked.

As TJ drove the van out of the parking lot Ernie jumped in through the open door and Rick slammed it shut. "Damn straight. And might I add it's pretty much the best plan ever."

"Not bad, Rick. Now shut your pie hole," snapped TJ.

Rick whispered, "He doesn't like his call sign."

Mike cradled Axe's head on his lap. "Guys, you're the best."

"You're not going to cry are you?" asked Rick.

"Rick, shut your pie hole," Mike said.

Twenty minutes later, Axe was sleeping on a duvet at the end of Mike's bed as the men discussed the dog's future over a beer in the living room.

"What's your plan now you've got him here?" TJ asked as he sucked back a *Coors*.

Mike let his shoulders drop as he sat on the couch. "I

guess I'm gonna have to do something about his temperament or I won't be able to leave him with anyone when
we're on jobs."

"So you're going to keep him?" asked Rick.

"I can't trust him with anyone else."

"You need to take him to the vet I told you about. She'll
sort him out," said Ernie.

Rick grinned. "Any luck–"

"Pie hole, Rick," said TJ.

Laughter filled the room as Mike took a swig from his
beer. For the first time since Axe had been shot he felt hopeful. "OK, I'll take him in to see her first thing tomorrow. TJ,
do you mind if I'm a little late for work."

"Take the day off."

"What about us?" Rick asked.

"Ernie can have a late start. You and I are going
running, got to burn off all that pie you've been shoving in
your hole."

"Well, this is it, bud." Mike opened the passenger door of
his pickup and lifted Axe out. He carried the wounded dog
across a dusty parking lot into the waiting room of the Iron
Canyon Veterinary Clinic.

A female receptionist looked up and smiled. "Hi."

"Hi. We're here to see Doctor Alison Taylor."

"Perfect timing. Her last patient finished up early so you
can take him straight through."

"Thanks." Mike pushed the door open with his foot and
carried Axe into the examination room.

Doctor Taylor greeted him with a bright smile. "Hello.
You can put him down over there." She gestured to a table.

Mike saw immediately why Ernie's brother thought she was cute. A brunette with a button nose, lush mouth and green eyes, she wasn't what he'd call a stunner but more the girl next door. He judged her height at around five-foot-six. Not short, but by no means tall. And, while she wore baggy scrubs, they couldn't hide her curvy figure. Not really his type, but then this wasn't about him.

"Mike, isn't it?"

"Yeah, you must be Alison."

She nodded as she washed her hands. "On the phone you said he was shot?"

Mike kept a close eye on Axe as the dog surveyed the room, every muscle tense. "Correct, he's a Military Working Dog. Discharged as a result of the injury."

"And it was a little over two weeks ago?"

"Yes, he's recovering well but–"

"His temperament has changed?" Alison added as she dried her hands.

Mike nodded.

"I see that a lot with heavy trauma. I get a lot of dogs with PTSD from being hit by cars or attacked by another animal." She approached Axe. "OK handsome, let's have a look at you."

The dog's ears flattened against his skull and he bared his teeth.

"Axe, no!"

Alison lifted a hand to silence Mike. "It's fine. He's just letting me know he's not happy. You'd never bite me would you, Axe?"

Her question was answered with another savage growl.

Mike frowned. "Axe! Look, I'm not so sure about that. I wouldn't–"

"No, it's OK. Mike, it might be better if you waited outside. Axe seems to be taking a lot of his cues from you."

His eyes narrowed. "What are you saying?"

"I'm saying you've been as traumatized as he has. You're tense and worried. Totally understandable, but your energy isn't helping the situation."

"Now hang on a second. I'm a qualified dog handler. We've been working together for three years. If anyone understands how he feels, it's me."

She nodded. "That's exactly my point. Listen, I don't mind if you stay. But I want you to sit down over there and keep quiet." She pointed to a chair against the wall.

He slumped into the seat and crossed his arms.

"Let's try again, Axe." The vet took a liver treat from a jar and extended it on her open palm. "Are you going to be a good boy?"

The dog glanced at Mike but he ignored him.

Alison took a step closer. "Good boy, Axe." Slowly, inch-by-inch, she made her way closer. The dog's nostrils flared as he inhaled the scent of the dried meat. When she was close enough, his tongue shot out and scooped it off her palm.

"Tasty isn't it?"

Alison was now standing less than a foot from the dog. He eyed her suspiciously as he chewed the snack.

Mike bit his tongue as she reached out to pat his head. He saw the dog's lip lift in a half growl.

She displayed no fear, instead ruffled his ears. "Hey now, none of that."

Mike watched with growing disbelief as Axe let the vet inspect his wound without growling. "I'll be damned," he murmured.

The dog remained silent but watched Alison's every move.

"You're healing well, handsome man," she patted his head again. "Mike, can you put him on the ground so I can see how he walks."

He shook his head. "He can't walk, he's still wounded."

The vet's lips thinned. "Has he tried?"

"Look, I'm not a complete fool. I've had a few years experience with dogs and I don't think he's ready."

She raised her eyebrows. "And I guess my seven years of study and five in practical experience counts for nothing?"

Mike rolled his eyes. "Fine." He gently lifted Axe from the table and placed him on the floor.

The dog lay still on the tiles, his injured leg extended at an awkward angle.

Mike slumped back in the chair. "See."

Alison shook her head and took another treat from the jar. Squatting a few yards in front of Axe, she offered it to him. "Hey buddy, do you want this?"

His ears angled forward and his tail thumped the floor. His floppy ear bounced up and down.

Mike smiled. "Come on boy," he murmured.

Axe glanced at him, and then at the treat, and back to his partner. Then, with little effort, he climbed to his feet, walked forward and gently took it from her hand.

Mike didn't miss how he kept the wounded leg hitched high.

"Good boy." Alison ruffled his ears again. "Now let's go for a little walk." She took a lead from a hook on the wall, clipped it to his collar and led him slowly around the room.

Mike caught the dog's eye as they turned and walked back toward him. "Traitor," he mouthed. "So what do you think?" he asked gruffly, folding his arms.

"I think he's a beautiful animal who needs a little care. But most importantly, you need to stop treating him like a person."

It was Mike's turn to frown. "I don't treat him like a person."

"Listen, I know you've been through a lot with Axe. But he doesn't need your sympathy. He needs your leadership. He needs you to be strong, to tell him what to do."

Mike slumped back in the chair and closed his eyes. For a split second, he was transported back to Mexico, back to the moment when Axe was shot. If he had moved a little faster, he might have been able to save the dog from being wounded. It was a moment he had relived repeatedly since that day.

"Mike, Mike."

Alison's voice snapped him back to the present.

"Are you alright?"

"Yeah. Sorry, I spaced out. Yes, I hear you." He focused on Alison and realized she was watching him closely.

"Mike, how would you feel about Axe staying here at the clinic? Only for a week or two. You seem to have a lot on your mind and he would really benefit from intensive therapy. You could come and see him every day."

Mike nodded. "That would be good. I've got to work."

Her beaming smile instantly made him hopeful. Things would work out. Axe would be healed and maybe, just maybe, they'd be a team again. He said his farewells to the dog, then set up an account with the vet's assistant on his way out. As he pushed open the door to leave, he almost ran into a middle-aged blonde and two young children. "Morning, ma'am." He held open the door as the family passed through, then was on his way.

"Who the hell is that?" Leonie asked Alison when she joined her sister in the waiting area.

"Just a guy with an injured dog. How have you been?"

"I think you mean 'a total hunk' with an injured dog. You should definitely hit that."

Alison laughed. "Can you get your mind out of the gutter?" She glanced out the window as Mike climbed into his truck.

"Not when it's led there by an ass like that. So what's his story?"

"He's arrogant, over-confident and military. Not my type at all." She squatted to embrace her nieces.

"Handsome, fit, confident and a dog guy. No, you're right. He doesn't sound anything like your type."

"He's got issues, Leonie. Now, where do you want to go for brunch?"

"Perfect, you're always saving strays and you could do wonders with him."

She tucked one squealing child under each arm and hoisted the toddlers off the ground. "I'm a veterinarian, not a psychologist."

"Oh please. Men and dogs have so much in common. All they need is a pat, good food and—"

"Enough, you don't recall the date with Brian? Like I said, I'm staying the hell away from men."

Leonie grinned. "Come on, I mean a celibate nun would make an exception for that fine looking piece of—"

"Enough already, I'm starving."

As Mike drove through the security checkpoint at Coronado Naval Base his new phone chimed with a message. He pulled into the parking lot in front of the team rooms and glanced at the screen.

The old man wants to see you... TJ

Exiting his truck, Mike ducked inside and put on a clean uniform before heading over to the headquarters building.

"He's in his office," said Mack from behind his desk.

Mike continued down the corridor and knocked on the commander's door.

"Enter."

As he stepped inside, the CO glanced up from his computer and gestured to the seat opposite. Mike sat and prepared himself for the bombardment of questions regarding the abduction of Axe.

"How's things, Mike?"

"You know how it is, sir."

"Yeah, well I'm afraid I've got bad news and good news."

More than a little confused, Mike frowned. The commander was smart enough to recognize he was involved in the kidnap. Hell, until Doctor Taylor, Axe hadn't let anyone else near him except the squad members. Mike swallowed hard and met the commander's steely gaze.

"I'm not sure if you've heard but last night there was a break-in at the Miramar vet clinic. Kids looking for drugs busted in and now Axe is missing. That's the bad news."

Mike didn't know whether to feign surprise or anger.

"Did they catch them?"

Conner shook his head. "No, but the Jarhead Commander of the base assures me they'll find Axe. I wanted to let you know before you heard any rumors."

"Appreciate that, sir."

"The good news is with Axe missing we've got more time to appeal his discharge and destruction. I've nominated him for a heroism award. That should assist the process. Now, if he could just stay 'lost' for a week or three that should give us enough time."

Mike wasn't sure what to say. He swallowed the lump in his throat and fumbled for words. "Sir, I–"

"It's all good, son. As far as I'm concerned that dog's as important as any of my SEALs. In fact I'd swap him for half of Bravo Platoon. Their antics have caused me nothing but grief this week. Now, get out my office so I can sort out this shit storm."

As Mike left the headquarters and walked back to the team room he was filled with hope. Between Doctor Taylor, his squad, and now the commander there was a good chance Axe would be fine. Hell, if Conner had his way, the dog would become a decorated hero.

Entering the team room he found TJ and the others inspecting new marksman rifles.

Rick greeted him with a grin. "Hey brother, did you hear the news?"

"Yeah, allegedly Axe escaped from death row." Mike smiled.

"Our furry friend's going to be a decorated war hero," added TJ.

Mike blinked back tears and cleared his throat. "The only reason he's still alive is because of you guys. In fact this is the second time Rick's saved him."

"Don't mention it, he's a team-mate. Now, how about you give us the details on this sexy vet?"

He shook his head. "Always thinking with your dick, Rick. She knows her stuff. Axe is going to be staying with her for a few weeks."

Rick grinned. "Damn, she must be hot if you're letting her look after your dog."

"She's attractive, but not my type."

"Not your type," said Ernie. "You mean she doesn't have fake boobs and she's not going to steal all your shit?" He and Rick burst into laughter.

TJ handed Mike one of the marksman rifles. "OK, enough shit talking. Let's get these bad boys down to the range."

Chapter Five

Spots of rain fell from a gray sky as Vicente Barbosa leaned over his brother's coffin and gently straightened the dead man's tie. "I am alive today, Juan, because you saved my life. I swear on my soul that I will find the man who took yours. I will tear his heart from his chest and grind it under my boot." He wiped a tear from the corner of his eye before turning to face the crowd that had come to pay tribute to the brother of the Butcher.

Maneuvering through the people he shook hands, while forcing a smile, and nodded as they offered their sympathies. Once clear of the mourners, he weaved through the tombstones to the convoy of black SUVs parked at the edge of the cemetery. A dozen heavily armed guards waited for him. Until vengeance was his, Barbosa wasn't taking any chances. If the Americans wanted to kill him they would need to send more than a handful of SEALs.

"Where is Raul?" he asked as he reached the convoy.

His head of security rounded one of the SUVs. "Here."

Barbosa glanced at a vehicle climbing the track toward

them as he reached into his jacket, withdrew a handkerchief and wiped the raindrops from his aviator sunglasses. "Do you know who killed my brother?"

Raul shook his head. "No, we're still reviewing the CCTV footage."

The approaching vehicle pulled in behind his SUVs. A moment later five men dressed in dark suits and sunglasses exited. Barbosa's security detail eyeballed them as they approached and positioned themselves a few yards away.

He glared at his head of security. "They're with us. You've had eight days and still nothing?"

"We know they're SEALs."

The corner of Barbosa's lip curled into a snarl. "I told you that, you idiot." He reached into his jacket again as the party of suits arrived.

One of the men stepped forward, removing his sunglasses. His jet black eyes locked on to Barbosa's. The thin mustache crowning the man's upper lip trembled as he struggled to contain his mirth at the situation. "Mr. Barbosa."

He gave the man a curt nod and turned to his men with his hand still in his jacket. "This is Ramirez. He will be avenging Juan."

Raul scowled. "You're letting an outsider handle our business? Boss, that's—"

Barbosa drew a suppressed pistol and shot him neatly in the heart. His former head of security was dead before his body hit the wet grass.

He glared at his men. "Raul failed me. He wasn't there when my brother was killed, and then couldn't find me the man who murdered him." He spat at the body. "Failure will not be tolerated. Ramirez, if you please." He gestured to his armored SUV and his guards opened the door.

As they sped away Barbosa drummed his fingers against a leather armrest, eyeing Ramirez. "What have you discovered?"

"I've examined the CCTV footage and the man who shot your brother is a SEAL. A member of Team Five. They're based at Coronado, California."

"How do you know that?"

"A number of them wore patches on their shoulders." He held up his fingers in the V for victory symbol. "The Roman numeral five."

Barbosa took his pistol from his jacket and removed the suppressor. "Where exactly is Coronado?"

"Across the border in San Diego."

"And you have people there?"

"Yes."

"Good." He slid the weapon back into its holster and placed the warm suppressor in his pocket. "I want you to find the man who killed my brother. Then, when you do. I want you to kill someone he loves... before you bring me his heart."

Ramirez nodded. "This type of work is what I do best, Mr. Barbosa."

Chapter Six

Mike visited Axe every afternoon. Slowly, day by day, as the week progressed, he noticed a change in the dog's temperament. He'd gone from intermittently growling at Alison whenever she approached to allowing her to manipulate his injured leg with barely a whimper. By Thursday afternoon, Axe greeted Mike at the door of the recovery room with his lead in his mouth.

Alison gave him a smile. "He's been ready for the last hour. I think he wants you to take him for a walk."

Grinning, he took the lead from Axe's mouth, then shot her a concerned look. "You sure he's alright to walk outside?"

Stepping closer she placed her hand on his elbow. "Mike, Axe isn't a child. He's a dog. He'll be fine."

He smiled sheepishly. "I know, he's also my best friend. Makes it easy to forget." His eyes lingered on hers for a moment. Then she realized that she was holding his arm and blushed.

"You guys have fun."

As he walked Axe down the corridor, to the exercise yard, the dog kept glancing back at Alison. "You really like her don't you?" It wasn't something he could ever say about Stacey. Axe and the former model had been standoffish from day one.

The dog paused at the door and looked back at the recovery room.

"Come on, we'll see her again in a bit."

Once in the yard they strolled along the fence. Axe responded well on the lead but still protected his wounded leg. Ernie's Mom was right. Alison was a miracle worker. It had been barely two weeks since Axe had been shot and here he was walking.

After a few laps of the tennis court-sized yard Axe had warmed up and tentatively tried using his injured leg.

Remembering what Alison had said about leadership he began running him through the drills they used at work.

He started simple, walking backward with the dog staying by his side. Then he removed the lead and allowed Axe to wander the yard by himself.

"Axe, freeze."

The dog stopped instantly.

"Axe, come."

He limped to Mike and sat in front of him. He slapped his thigh and the dog walked clockwise around him and sat alongside his left leg.

"Good boy." He bent, ruffled his ears, and fished in his pocket for a treat.

"You two work so well together," said Alison from the back door of the clinic. "Coffee?" She held out a mug while sipping from another.

Mike turned and flashed a smile. "Um, what have you done to my dog?"

"What do you mean?"

"He's changed completely. He's back to normal."

Axe barked excitedly and walked toward the veterinarian.

Mike followed the dog and took the coffee that Alison offered him. "OK, so aside from being in love with you, he's back to normal."

She leaned and tussled Axe's ears. "It's nice having the attention of a handsome man like you."

Mike smiled as he sat next to her on the stairs. "So where to from here?"

"We've still got a bit of work to do. While his leg is healing well, the PTSD has a little way to go. Isn't that right, handsome?"

Axe was looking up at her admiringly with his long tongue lolling out of the side of his mouth.

"Hey, cut that out. You're going to give me a complex." Mike took a toy from his pocket, squeezed it and threw it across the lawn.

They watched Axe limp after it.

He took a sip of the coffee and held the mug with both hands. "Hey look, I was a bit of a jerk earlier this week. I want to apologize for that." He turned and looked at her.

"Don't worry about it. I know I came across a little harsh."

Their gaze locked over their mugs and Mike noted how pretty her green eyes were. There was a kindness about them that he hadn't noticed before. His gaze dropped to her supple lips and he imagined kissing them. Then his eyes flicked back to hers. Her intensity confirmed a similar thought was on her mind.

Then, as he considered leaning across and kissing her, Axe dropped the now slobbery toy directly onto his groin.

"Thanks, bud." He laughed as he recovered the slimy ball. "As much as I hate to, I've got to get going." He finished the coffee with a single gulp and climbed to his feet. "Do you want me to take him inside?"

She shook her head, tossing her long brown hair. "No, I'll stay out here with him for a little longer. We'll see you tomorrow."

He patted the dog. "Be good, bud. I'll see you later." With a final nod and a smile he entered the clinic and made for the front door.

As he reached the waiting area, he heard, "Hey, Mike."

"Yeah." He turned to face Alison.

She looked as if she wanted to ask him a question but fumbled her words. "Umm, I just wanted to know what time to expect you?"

He smiled. "I'm hoping to finish up work early. If I can, it will be around fifteen hundred."

"That's three, right?"

"Yeah, three."

"See you then."

As Mike left, Alison slapped her forehead with her palm. Feeling Axe push past her leg, she glanced down at him. "You didn't see that, did you?"

He sat and stared at her.

"Oh, you did. Well that's even more embarrassing. Come on. Let's get you something to eat."

───────

Early the next morning, Mike joined his team-mates at a training facility. Located on the outskirts of San Diego and run by civilian contractors it was a state of the art shoot-house that allowed, low risk, and highly realistic indoor training.

He spotted TJ and the others standing behind one of the black minivans they used to transport equipment and personnel around town. The squad had almost finished gearing up for a session in the 'house'. They wore protective chemical warfare suits and were now strapping on their combat vests. As he approached, TJ broke away from the van and headed toward him.

Mike gave him a nod. "Hey, Chief."

"Morning, Mike, once you're ready grab the clowns and I'll see you inside."

"Roger." He continued across to the van where Rick and Ernie were preparing. "Good morning." Grinning he retrieved his gear bag from the trunk.

Rick met his smile with a scowl. "What's good about it? TJ's got us running drills in gas masks and suits. Gonna be sweating our asses off for the next five hours."

Mike pulled his protective clothing on over his T-shirt and shorts. "Yeah, but Rick it's a beautiful day."

"How's our boy doing?" Ernie asked as he opened a weapons crate and took out his carbine.

"Great. He's coming along well. Alison has done wonders with him." He slung his armor on over the protective suit. As he reached for his weapon, he caught both Rick and Ernie grinning at him. "What?"

Rick shot him a broad smirking grin. "So it's Alison now, is it? That's why you're so damn happy. You're hitting that aren't you, bud?"

Ernie's eyes narrowed. "My brother said she was hot."

"What? No. No, it's not like that. She's not my type." Mike avoided eye contact with his friends as he attached his weapon to the clip on his rig. "You guys ready?"

Picking up his gas mask, he walked in the direction of the shoot-house.

Rick yelled after him. "I call bullshit. Why else would you be so damn happy? Only time I'm wearing a shit-eating grin like that is after a night of hot, sweaty sex. Oh shit, you're not back with Stacey are you?"

Mike waved him off and pushed open the door into the training facility.

Already inside, TJ had his gas mask on and his weapon ready. "Game faces on boys. We're running room clearance drills."

Mike let his rifle hang and adjusted the straps on his mask. "Not everyone's a sex-crazed maniac like you, Rick. Some of us are high on life."

"You fuckers better mask up or you're gonna be high on tear gas," yelled TJ as he hit the gas release button.

A rotating red light flashed. A hissing noise filled the air as they fitted their masks.

"You like her though, don't you?" Rick wheezed through his respirator.

Mike inserted a magazine of paint cartridges into his weapon and cocked it. "She's cooler than I initially thought."

Gas was now visible inside the room.

"Just call me cupid," Ernie said, using his carbine as if it were a bow.

"I'll call you mother-fucking stupid," added Rick. "Boy needs to tap that, not get into another relationship."

"Wrong!" TJ bellowed through his mask. "You dimwits need to tap some goddamn targets otherwise I'm going to keep you in these suits all day."

Ernie readied his weapon. "No need to be like that."

"We're just looking out for our boy, TJ. I mean, we don't want to have to run a girlfriend selection course, just yet."

"What the... Are you in love, Mike?" demanded TJ.

"Negative, Chief!"

"Good, if that changes, let me know." TJ racked his weapon. "Now, let's put paint on paper. On me!"

Alison's favorite café was an eclectic establishment only five minutes from her clinic. A converted garage, the Spanner Shop now housed a four-head espresso machine and the best sandwiches and muffins in a ten-mile radius.

As she pushed the door open, a bell clanged. The twenty-something barista glanced up from the machine and smiled from under his handlebar mustache.

"Hi, Simon." Glancing around, she spotted her sister sitting at a table.

"The usual, Ali? Your sister has already ordered."

"Thanks. That would be lovely."

She wound her way through the rough-hewn benches and ambushed her sister with a hug and a kiss on the cheek. "Hello, beautiful lady."

"Beautiful?" Leonie returned the embrace. "I feel like I've been hit by a eighteen-wheeler."

Alison sat on the bench opposite.

"Whatever you do," continued Leonie, "don't have children. Especially not daughters, and in the name of all things sane, do not volunteer to help out at a damn ballet camp."

"Is that where the girls are?"

A waiter arrived with their coffees. "Here's your quad and a latte." He placed a gargantuan mug of coffee in front of Leonie. The smaller tumbler looked like a shot glass next to the bucket of caffeine.

"How many shots are in that?" Alison asked.

"Four," replied the waiter. "Enjoy."

"Leonie, you're going to give yourself a heart attack."

"Trust me when I say it will be welcomed." She wrapped her hands around the mug and took a sip. "God I needed this. Now, tell me what's been happening in your life?"

"Work, work and more work."

"Any more hunky Navy SEALs been to visit?"

Alison shrugged as she sipped.

"Oh, he's been back hasn't he?"

"He kind of has to, Leonie, I'm treating his dog. He comes in every day to visit Axe."

Her sister smirked. "I don't think I could handle that. I would have torn those jeans off him by now and had my way with him on every horizontal surface in the clinic."

Alison snorted coffee from her nose. "You're out of control." She reached for a napkin.

"No, you're out of control. Big hunky man who looks like he's straight off a *Calvin Klein* poster comes in and you do nothing. You have to hit him up for a date."

"You want me to ask him out?"

"Um yeah, this is the teens. Or whatever the hell they call this decade. You know what I mean. We're all empowered and shit now. You can ask any guy out if you want to. Hell if you want to bang him on the first date that's completely up to you."

As she wiped coffee from her chin, Alison caught the annoyed glance of another patron. "Shh, I want to come back here." She giggled.

Leonie shrugged. "I'm just saying it's OK for you to ask

him out. Hell, bring him here and have a coffee. Or, are you still hung up on him being a jerk."

"Well—"

"God, Ali, you don't have to shag his personality just that rock solid body."

"No, it isn't that. He's actually turned out be a decent guy. Yeah, he's a little stubborn and full of himself. But the way he is with Axe is really very sweet. He's so gentle and kind, yet also stern. The two of them work perfectly together, like a finely-tuned machine. He's also a really good listener—"

"Wow, you're already in love with the guy. You should just get down on one knee and SEAL the deal," Leonie said between chuckles.

Alison blushed and lifted her coffee, hoping it hid her flushed cheeks.

"Don't be shy, sis. If you like the guy, ask him out. Hell, make it about the dog if you want. Get to know him and then…" She made a circle with her fingers and inserted the opposite hand's index finger. "Uh huh. Oh yeah."

"You're shocking."

Leonie cocked her head to one side. "And you're in need of a good lay."

She checked her watch then downed the last of her coffee. "Sorry this was quick, but I've got to get back to the clinic. I've got a client coming in to check on a dog. Let's do something together, real soon." She jumped up and gave her sister another hug.

"You're leaving me for him, aren't you?"

She kissed her on the cheek and started for the door.

"Fine, run off after your handsome Navy SEAL and leave me to cry into my bucket of coffee," Leonie yelled across the café.

"Oh god, I'm so sorry," Alison told the barista. "Please, put it all on my account and I'll fix it up when I'm next in."

"Good luck," he said winking.

She paused. "I'm going back to work."

"Sure you are."

Alison's assistant glanced up from her computer as she entered the clinic. "He's already out back with Axe. He's been here for the last hour." She pointed to a bright bunch of flowers on the counter. "And he brought these in for us."

"Really?"

"Alright, they might only be for you."

Alison suppressed her smile until she entered the corridor, then it burst free. She gathered herself, before stepping outside. In the exercise yard Mike and Axe were playing ball. She watched them for a few throws and noted the dog was still guarding his injured leg. Catching Mike's eye she called out, "He's definitely improved, but he still has a long way to go."

He flashed her a smile.

Alison caught herself staring. Mike was wearing a tight T-shirt that did little to hide his muscular build. His biceps strained at the thin fabric sending a shiver up her spine. Her sister was right. The tall, blonde-haired SEAL looked like he had stepped straight from a *Calvin Klein* shoot onto her lawn. The driver's license he'd used to open his account said he was 28. However, his slate gray eyes told a different story. They'd seen more than their fair share of pain and suffering.

He smiled, revealing a dimple, and she knew he'd caught her ogling, probably almost drooling.

"The improvements are all because of you. Two weeks ago the Army vet told me he might never walk again and couldn't be trusted around people. Now, look at him."

Axe lay on the grass, the ball still in his mouth as he watched them.

"Hey, what can I say? He's a special dog." Alison stepped closer, drawn in by his smile.

"You're an amazing vet, Alison, I'm so glad we found you and I don't think either of us will ever be able to thank you enough."

"Please, call me Ali, and the beautiful flowers are a great start."

He glanced down at his feet. "I… I just wanted to say thanks for taking such good care of my best friend."

Her heart lurched at his shyness.

They sat together on the rear deck.

Mike stared out into the distance. "He saved my life you know."

Glancing sideways at him, she spotted a tear in his eye as he watched the dog chew the ball.

"Guy got the drop on me, would've killed me. Axe took the bullet." He turned to face her. "That's not something you can ever repay. That's just one reason why I couldn't let them put him down."

She reached over, grasped his hand and squeezed it gently. "No one's going to hurt him now, Mike. He's safe here."

Sensing his distress, Axe abandoned his ball, walked across, and put his head on Mike's knee.

"See, there isn't a person in the world he trusts more than you."

He scratched behind Axe's floppy ear. "Even after everything I've put him through?"

"You guys are definitely a team."

"Yeah, well this team-mate has to get going." He gave her a heart-melting smile. "Thanks again, Ali. I guess I'll see you tomorrow?"

"I look forward to it."

He gave the dog one last pat, rose, and made for the door.

"Mike!"

He turned. "Yeah?"

She took a deep breath. "Tomorrow, after you visit Axe, would you like to grab a coffee or something?"

The corners of his mouth curved in an easy smile. "I'd like that. I'll be here around two. Does that work for you?"

"Don't you mean fourteen hundred?"

"It's a date." He disappeared through the door.

The dog looked up at her with intelligent eyes.

"You heard him," she gushed. "It's a date."

Chapter Seven

Ali's gaze met Mike's over their coffees. The pair had spent the past hour exercising Axe, then left him in the care of her assistant. Now they sat in her favorite coffee haunt, the Spanner Shop. She traced her finger around the lip of her cup. "So, why a SEAL?"

Mike shrugged. "My dad was a Navy guy. Always said it was the best time of his life. So when I left college, I decided to enlist. The recruiter was a team guy, and well, the rest is history. What about you, why a vet?"

"I grew up on a farm in the Midwest and always loved animals. There was no way I would or could do anything else."

He smiled. "Well, Axe and I are pretty happy you didn't take a different path."

Ali melted at the sight of his dimples. "I'm glad you found me. Axe is a wonderful dog. I'm enjoying working with him."

He held his mug in both hands and peered over it. "Uh huh."

She blushed. "Well… it's been nice getting to know you, too."

"I'm enjoying it." He lowered the mug. "So, why doesn't an intelligent, attractive woman like you have a man in her life?"

"What is it with you men? You all assume I want and need a man in my life. Why doesn't a hunky SEAL like you have a partner… or do you?"

He shook his head. "Nope, just me and Axe."

She laughed, tucking a stray strand of hair behind her ear. "I'm just messing with you, Mike. I've had a few relationships. But none of the guys hang around. I guess they don't like competing with dogs for attention."

"Hardly an even competition, is it?"

"What do you mean?"

"Well, dogs are loyal, steadfast, always happy to see you, no matter what. No man can compete with that."

"Are you saying I should date a Golden Retriever?"

"No, maybe just a man who has things in perspective."

"Oh." She raised an eyebrow, suggestively. "And do you have things in perspective, Mr. Michael Saunders?"

He smiled into his coffee. "Maybe. Oh, before I forget, is it alright if I take Axe out tomorrow?"

"He's your dog. You don't have to ask my permission."

"I just thought that, as his doctor you should be consulted," he said, his expression matching his serious tone.

"Well then, as his doctor I should probably know exactly what it is he'll be doing."

"Ah, that part's a surprise."

She frowned. "Well then, how can I know if it's suitable for his condition?"

He grinned. "Well, I thought you could supervise."

She set her coffee down. "Sounds like you're trying to sneak in a second date."

He leaned across the table, stopping when their lips were less than an inch apart. "That's exactly what I'm doing. I've got to run, but I'll pick you up tomorrow at ten."

"Yes, sir," she murmured, fighting the urge to kiss him.

"I'm not an officer, Ali. You don't have to call me sir."

She pursed her lips seductively. "What if I want to?"

"Now, that's a different matter altogether." He settled back in his chair and downed the last of his coffee. "I really do have to run. I'll pick you and Axe up at ten hundred sharp."

"I look forward to it."

Ali's gaze followed his every movement as he went to the counter and paid the bill. Her eyes were fixed on his buttocks. Damn, they looked good in the tight jeans he wore. He glanced back at her before disappearing through the door. She sighed as she finished her coffee. Crap, she hadn't asked Mike what to wear. A ten o'clock pickup with Axe suggested something physical, she hoped. Because the last thing she wanted to do was turn up in heels and a skirt when they were going on an adventure.

Outside the café, as Mike approached his truck, he spotted a white sedan across the street. His eyes narrowed as he studied it. The car was familiar. Too familiar, right down to the dented front right fender. He swore he had seen it earlier today, parked outside Ali's clinic. As he eyeballed the car, trying to make out the driver, it pulled out into traffic.

He drummed his fingers against his thigh as he watched

it disappear behind a sixteen wheeler. Shaking his head he opened his truck and climbed in. The coffee had left him a little edgy. Not to mention he hadn't been sleeping well since Axe was shot. He managed a smile as his mind turned to the date he'd planned. Now at least he had something to look forward to.

Chapter Eight

Ramirez located Barbosa perched on a bag of coffee beans, smoking a cigar at the rear of the rusted warehouse. A number of heavies stood in a semicircle around the elderly, battered, man crumpled at the Butcher's feet.

He didn't trouble himself with the victim. That wasn't his business. He was being paid to find Juan Barbosa's killer and exact revenge.

The cartel boss exhaled a mouthful of smoke into the face of his victim, before looking up. "You got something for me?"

Ramirez's eyes narrowed behind his aviator sunglasses. "Can we go somewhere private to talk?"

"No. I am comfortable here."

"That's not what concerns me."

Barbosa laughed. "Oh, don't worry about Pedro. Where he's going there's no one to talk or listen." He prodded the body with his shoe. "Isn't that right, my friend?"

Ramirez shrugged. "In that case, I've found your man."

"Who is he?"

"His name is Michael Saunders. He's a Petty Officer with SEAL Team Five. My people are gathering intelligence. When we have enough information, we'll strike."

Barbosa rose from his perch and signaled for Ramirez to walk with him, between shelves stacked high with fragrant coffee beans.

"I want you to find what this man loves. Gather every detail of his life and find what he lives for. Then, when you have done that, I want you to take it from him." Pivoting, Barbosa turned and placed a hand on his shoulder. "I want him to feel loss like I have felt. I want him to grieve like I have grieved. Then, when he begs for his life, I want you to kill him."

Chapter Nine

The next morning at 1035, Ali sat beside Mike as he drove his pickup across a cattle guard and up a dusty road. Ahead, a gleaming white mansion materialized from behind a line of trees.

Ali thought it looked like a temple, more at home in ancient Greece than California.

"Please tell me you haven't brought me to a country club when I'm wearing sneakers and leggings," she lamented as they approached the multi-story, white-pillared structure.

"Nope, you're good." Mike turned onto a track that weaved through the freshly mowed lawns and lush green gardens that skirted the mansion.

Ali twisted her head to look back at the house. "What is this place?"

"It's a country club for rich jerks. A buddy of mine's old man owns it. He lets me use the facilities."

The landscape dramatically turned from manicured gardens to the harsh, rocky canyons that Southern California was renowned for. The road snaked its way up a narrow valley for another half-mile before he parked the truck. "We're here."

Exiting the air-conditioned cabin, Ali inhaled a deep breath of warm, clean air, and surveyed their destination.

The valley was pristine desert with cactus, rocky outcrops, and stunted desert plants pockmarking the steep walls. Turning, she inspected the area behind the truck as Mike dropped the tailgate. It had been cleared out to about fifty yards, at which point there was a tall mound of sand.

"Mike, what is this place?" She joined him as he was unloading stakes with targets attached to them. "Ah, now it makes sense."

"Yep, we're going to do some shooting." He opened the rear doors of the dual-cab truck and lifted Axe from the bench seat to the ground. The dog immediately limped around to the tailgate and sat next to Ali. "Buddy, I'm beginning to think you prefer her over me."

"Well, I have been feeding him and you know that's the quickest way to a man's heart."

"So I've heard."

Stroking Axe's head she watched as Mike set up two targets, twenty yards from the pickup in front of the wall of sand. Then he took a locked box from the cabin and opened it, revealing a black handgun. "You ever fired a pistol?"

Ali shook her head. "No. My dad wasn't really a gun kind of guy."

"That's cool. It takes all types." Mike took up the pistol. "This is a Glock nine millimeter. It's the most common pistol used by police and military. Easy to use and very safe if treated with respect."

He spent the next fifteen minutes explaining how the pistol worked and how to manipulate the controls. Then using an empty magazine, he taught her how to load, cock and position herself to shoot. When she was confident he took a live magazine, loaded the pistol and positioned her facing the targets.

"Don't be afraid of the weapon, Ali. Treat it with respect and never forget that you're the one in complete control."

She held the pistol in both hands, how he had shown her, and aimed at one of the paper targets. Squeezing the trigger, she flinched as the weapon fired. Dust spurted from the ground below the target. She lowered the pistol to her side. "I'm afraid I'm not very good at this."

"Hey, it's your first time." Mike turned and nodded at the truck where Axe was sitting calmly with his tongue lolling. "Axe, thinks you're doing OK."

Ali turned and checked the dog. "He's not afraid. That's a good sign."

"Not as tense as you. Now, let's try again." Mike stepped in behind her as she raised the handgun.

As he wrapped his arms around her and placed his hands on hers, a tingle of excitement raced across her skin. His body was hard and muscular and he smelt like sweat, oil, and aftershave. She swallowed and concentrated on the pistol's sights.

"See how you've got your arms locked out. You're all tense. You need to relax more."

That was verging on impossible, she thought. His mouth was directly next to her ear and she could feel his breath on the side of her face. A tremor of desire rippled through her as his lips gently brushed her lobe. She exhaled, tried to relax, and gently squeezed the trigger.

Dust spat up from the mound, slightly to the left of the target.

"Nearly there."

Yes I am, she thought. She forced herself to relax, trying to ignore the sensation of his body pressed against hers as she aligned the pistol with the target.

"You want to focus on moving just your finger tip," he said softly.

"You're making it kind of hard to concentrate." She squeezed the trigger and the pistol jumped. "Where did that go?" she asked, lowering the gun.

"On target." He took the pistol from her, cleared it and they walked downrange.

She joined him as he examined the paper. "I can't see where it hit."

"In the black." He pointed to a bullet hole half an inch under the bullseye. "Nice one, sharpshooter, you're a natural."

She leaned forward and poked the mark with her finger. "Woo hoo." Straightening she turned and found herself looking directly into Mike's eyes. For a moment they gazed at each other and for a split second, she thought he would kiss her. Then he faltered and turned his attention back to the target.

"Do you want another go?"

She nodded. "Yes."

As they walked back to the firing point she wondered if Mike was suffering similar emotional wounds to Axe. It made sense, considering the bond between the two. She noticed the dog watching his every move as he thumbed cartridges into the pistol's magazine.

He handed it to her with the pistol. "This time I want you to try it by yourself."

She took them tentatively and turned to face the mound. "Make sure I don't do anything wrong." She inserted the magazine and pulled back the slide, as he had shown her. A smile confirmed it was correct. Then she took careful aim and squeezed the trigger.

"On target."

She fired again.

"OK, so you've definitely got the hang of this. Most people take at least an hour before they're hitting the paper."

Smiling she lowered the pistol. "I put it down to a great instructor."

"Nope, you're a natural." Mike loaded another magazine and handed it to her. "Must be the doctor's steady hands."

She fired off another four magazines before calling it quits.

"I've got something to admit to you," Mike said as they walked back to the truck.

Ali's eyes narrowed. "Is this where you tell me you're married?"

He laughed. "No, nothing like that. It's just… It wasn't my intention to only teach you to shoot." He lifted the truck's tonneau cover and hauled out a picnic basket and a cooler. "I planned on wooing you with champagne and fine food."

She smiled. "And here's me, swooning after one bullseye. I really should learn how to play hard to get."

Mike spread a blanket on the ground. As he laid out the food he shot her a worried look. "Now, we've got cold chicken and a selection of salads. I hope that's OK. I asked your assistant what you liked and if there was anything you didn't eat. She said you love fried chicken. That was OK, wasn't it?"

Dumbstruck, she nodded. "Are all SEALs so thoughtful?"

He grinned. "No ma'am, we just like to be prepared. Time spent on recon is seldom wasted."

"Well, I think it is exceptionally sweet."

Their gazes met and held as Mike moved closer and placed a hand on the side of her hip.

She closed her eyes in anticipation.

With an excited bark, Axe nudged them both with a wet nose.

Mike let his hand drop. "I think he can smell the chicken."

She managed a weak smile. "We can't have him going hungry."

Mike sat in the web seats of a C-130 transport and adjusted his parachute leg straps. It was Monday morning and the squad was conducting free-fall insertion training. Decked out in camouflage uniforms they wore bulky parachutes, heavy packs and their weapons were strapped to the sides of their bodies.

The roar of the aircraft's engines almost drowned out Rick's voice. "How was the weekend, brother?"

Mike shot him thumbs-up. "Good, real good."

"Did you bang the vet?"

"Rick, she saved the life of a team-mate. Show a bit of respect." He returned his attention to checking his equipment.

"You totally did, didn't you?"

"Rick, have you ever heard the expression 'a gentleman never tells'?"

"Bro, you're a SEAL. So that's clearly not you. Cough up the details. Was she a rocket?"

Mike shook his head. "You're a child, Rick. Ali's more of a woman than you could comprehend."

"He's got a point there," added Ernie from where he was conducting his own checks. "You've got simpler tastes, Rick."

"Whatever, we all know Mike's hitting it."

"How about you clowns keep your minds on the job," bellowed TJ from where he stood next to the controls for the aircraft's ramp. He lifted two gloved fingers. "Two minutes out."

"You totally had a dirty weekend with her, didn't you?" Rick continued.

Mike fastened his oxygen mask and pulled his goggles over his eyes. The others did the same and they joined TJ at the ramp.

"Stand by," he transmitted over their internal frequency. "Oxygen on."

They turned their tanks on. A moment later, the ramp lowered with a whine. Icy cold air ripped into the cargo hold.

"Thirty seconds," said TJ.

"I bet Mike didn't last that long," transmitted Rick.

"Pie hole, Rick." TJ held up his hand.

They readied themselves. "Go, go, go!"

Mike leaped off the ramp into the thin air, alongside the Chief. Rick and Ernie were close behind.

As they tracked across the clear sky Mike stabilized himself. At close to thirty thousand feet, San Diego bay was a sparkling jewel. The bright, blue water stood out against the golden beaches and slate-gray cityscape.

"Hey, Mike," Rick transmitted.

He turned his head and was faced with the sight of Ernie in an all-fours position with Rick behind him, one hand behind his head and the other on Ernie's hip.

"Is this how you did it, bud? Doggy style with the vet."

Mike couldn't believe what he was seeing as the two veteran SEALs pretended to fornicate while free-falling at an altitude close to twenty-thousand feet.

"Seriously, show a bit of respect guys."

"What the hell are you clowns doing?" transmitted TJ. "Tighten up the formation."

Mike shook his head as the pair abandoned their pantomime and joined him and TJ in a diamond shape.

"Mike," transmitted TJ.

"Yeah?"

"Things getting serious with this girl?"

He didn't respond as they plummeted through the atmosphere at 120 miles per hour.

"You know what's got to happen if it is, brother. Approaching two thousand."

Mike checked his altimeter. As the needle hit two thousand feet he pulled his chute. The canopy expanded overhead, the harness wrenching at his shoulders. Then, as he leveled out, he checked that the rest of the squad was safely under silk.

"OK, form up on me," ordered TJ.

He steered his chute in behind the Chief.

"Mike, you didn't answer the question. You serious about this girl, or what?"

Mike didn't respond.

"Silence is damning, isn't it TJ?" Rick said.

"You wouldn't know, Rick. You can't keep your pie hole shut. Now, what's the deal with this girl?"

Mike drew on his right toggle, banking to follow the Chief. "Yeah, I like her. She's done wonders for Axe. She's also nothing like any other woman I've met." Their drop zone on the beach was rapidly approaching.

"Good for you. Keep us posted on how it's progressing."

Mike flared as the sand rose toward him, and touched down gently a dozen feet from TJ. He pivoted and watched Rick and Ernie make their landings.

"Good work guys," TJ bellowed. "Now let's dump these chutes and hit the range."

Chapter Ten

Ramirez was sitting with his family at the dinner table when his phone rang. He pulled the device from his pocket and inspected it.

"You know the rules. No business at dinner," his wife said.

"This is important."

She frowned, but dismissed him with a wave of her hand.

"Thank you, darling." Leaving the dining area, he answered the call as he entered the living room. "Speak!"

"Boss, it's me, Eduardo."

"What have you got?"

"I've been following this guy for a week now. Every day he goes to a veterinary clinic in Iron Canyon."

"Why?"

"I think he's seeing the woman who works there. They've been spending a lot of time together with a dog."

Ramirez grabbed a packet of cigarettes from the coffee table. "So, our target has a woman. That's good."

"It would be easy to grab her."

He tucked the phone between his shoulder and ear, and tapped a cigarette into his palm. "Not yet. Keep watching. I need to get our people in place."

"You got it, boss."

Terminating the call, he scooped a lighter off the table and strode outside to smoke. Lighting up, he gazed out over the wide expanse of desert dusted with saltbush and cacti. Sunset bathed the harsh landscape in a soft orange hue that masked its true nature. He exhaled. It was a lot like the happy family life he maintained with his wife.

As he smoked the howl of a coyote filled the air. Within a matter of moments another joined the first animal's call. He smiled as he listened to their chorus.

Once he finished the cigarette, he flicked it off the porch into the sand and punched a number into his phone. "Pedro, we're going to need two vehicles, eight men and clean passports with US visas."

"What's the mission?"

"We're going to take care of a problem for our good friend."

"So, it will pay well."

"Of course. I want the best we have."

"When do you need them ready?"

He stroked his mustache as he considered the question. "Twenty-four hours."

"Done."

Terminating the call, he considered another cigarette when a voice startled him.

"Are you going to finish dinner with your family?"

His wife's tone implied it was not a question. "Yes, my dear."

"What was the call about?" she asked as she led him back into the house.

"Business, darling. I may have to leave, later in the week."

"How long? Remember, your son's football final is this weekend."

Ramirez took his seat at the head of the table. "A few days at most. It's a simple in and out job."

Wearing a one-piece swimsuit, Ali stood in the portable rehabilitation spa set up in the yard. She watched as Mike led Axe, in a bright yellow vest that resembled a lifejacket, toward the spa.

"Ali, I'm not sure this is going to work."

"Why?"

"He hates water."

She placed her hands on her hips and cocked her head. "That information would have been useful yesterday."

Mike smiled but his eyes never left her curvaceous frame. The plain, one-piece suit did little to hide her curves.

"Hey sailor, how about we focus on rehab and not the merchandise."

As he lifted his gaze back to hers he caught the smile on her lips. With a grunt he picked up the dog and lowered him into the spa. "Your call. But, he's not going to like it."

Growling, Axe laid his ears flat and struggled.

Mike stepped back from the water and put him down on the grass. "See. I told you."

Ali folded her arms and arched an eyebrow, her lips pressed firmly together.

"Mike, he's a dog. He doesn't get to decide what's good for him, that's your job."

"Fine."

He lifted Axe over the lip of the spa and placed him in the warm water. The dog's legs cycled as they broke the surface, his ears flat against his skull as he paddled frantically.

Ali held him as he attempted to swim for the edge of the pool. "It's OK, Axe."

Mike leaned against the tub. "So what's this supposed to achieve?"

"He's guarding his damaged muscles resulting in atrophy. This will let him exercise them to their full potential, without weight."

"Making them stronger?"

"Yes."

Axe looked anything but strong as he panicked and tried to hook his legs over the side of the tub.

"I think he would be more comfortable if you held him." Ali struggled to keep him inside the hydro bath.

"I told you."

With a scowl, she snapped, "Michael, get in the tub."

"Yes ma'am." He stripped off his shirt.

It was Ali's turn to gawk. She knew SEALs trained hard but this was ridiculous. Every inch of his bronzed body looked like it had been chiseled from rock.

Climbing into the tub in his shorts, he stood alongside Ali in the warm water. Grasping Axe's vest, Mike pulled him back from the lip of the spa, forcing him to float. "Hey bud, it's OK."

Axe fought the water for a moment then adopted a powerful swimming stroke. Mike struggled to keep him in the middle of the tub.

Ali gave him a pat. "Not so bad, is it handsome.'

"Yeah, it's alright."

She glared sideways at him. "I wasn't talking to you."

He grinned. "Oh, my bad."

They stood side by side in the water as Axe continued to swim powerfully. It took the two of them to stop him reaching the side of the tub.

"Damn, he's strong," Mike grunted.

"This will make him even stronger."

Together they held the dog as he paddled at a steady pace.

"Is Axe your first military dog?" she asked.

"No, I had a dog before him…"

"And?"

"He was an explosives-detection dog. We were on a mission in Afghanistan. When we made entry on a Taliban stronghold he sniffed out an IED. He saved a lot of lives that day." Mike swallowed. "Most of us got clear, but when the bomb went off, Captain was on top of it."

"I'm so sorry," whispered Ali.

A tear ran down his cheek. "Two dogs have saved my life, Ali. I couldn't save Captain, but I can save Axe."

The compassion in her face was not something he'd ever seen in any of the women he had dated, certainly not in Stacey. Leaning over he kissed her gently on the lips. She responded tenderly, their mouths pressed softly together.

Mike's anguish was washed away in a sea of passion as her mouth opened slightly and he nibbled gently on her full, lower lip. He released Axe and slid his hand behind her head as the kiss gained in intensity. Their tongues touched and everything outside the kiss ceased to exist.

A bark quelled their passion. They broke apart, laughing as Axe barked again.

Mike turned his attention back to the dog. He ruffled Axe's ears. "I guess he thinks he should be the center of attention."

She smiled. "He seems to be pretty comfortable in the water."

"Well, technically he's a SEAL."

"Look, Mike," she said softly. "I've been hurt before—"

Mike grasped her around the waist and pulled her close. Pushing a strand of hair from her face, he kissed her again. There was no warm up this time. For a precious few minutes, he felt like he was a teenager. Then, Axe once more, voiced his displeasure.

Mike pulled back slightly. "I think he might have had enough." He gave her one long final kiss. Then, grateful that his shorts hid his excitement, he climbed out of the tub. Together they managed to lift the waterlogged dog out of the spa and onto the grass. Then, when he removed the float vest, Axe snorted and shook, covering him in wet strands of fur.

"Thanks, now I smell as bad as you do." He laughed as the dog rolled onto his back and wriggled like a furry worm. Then he jumped to his feet and trotted around the yard. "He looks better already."

Ali climbed out of the pool. "A few more sessions and you'll see a different dog." Wrapping a towel around her hips, she asked, "Do you want to have a shower before you go?"

He shook his head. "I'd love to. But, I've got to run. I'll get into clean clothes at work." He caught the flash of disappointment on her face. "Hey, I was wondering if you're free for dinner tomorrow night."

She wrinkled her nose. "Are you asking me out? Because I don't want things to get weird between us."

He grinned. "Yes. Yes, I am. Although, technically it's our third date. Look, I really like you Ali and I want to see where this goes. We can take it slow."

She returned the smile. "That sounds good."

———————

Mike was making adjustments to his equipment when Rick joined him inside the submarine lockout chamber. He glanced up and gave the Corpsman a nod. Like Mike he was dressed in a black wetsuit, scuba tanks, and a combat vest.

"You're spending a lot of time with this girl, brother. You telling me you still haven't squared her away?"

"I'm not telling you anything."

Rick adjusted his equipment. "Come on, Mike, we're supposed to be a team."

"Quit it. I'm not going to kiss and tell." He checked that his dive mask was secure around his neck.

"You hear that? Our boy's in love," Rick announced as TJ and Ernie joined them in the chamber.

"You falling for the dog doctor, *essé*?" asked Ernie as he spun the handle that sealed the men in the chamber.

"Guys, Ali's cool, I like her. But for now that's it."

TJ fixed him with a questioning look. "Like! That sounds awfully close to love, Romeo."

Mike shook his head. "I give up. You guys are out of control."

The three members of his squad burst into laughter.

"Commencing flood up and equalization," said Mike as he hit the button for the valve that released seawater into the chamber. "Watch your ears."

The men were still laughing as salt water rose rapidly to their knees.

"I'm in love. Boom, I'm all shook up," sang Rick until he had to stuff his regulator into his mouth. He continued humming until the water rose to the ceiling.

Mike gave all three men thumbs-up before he turned the locking arm and opened the outer door. They finned out onto the sleek black hull of the Virginia-class attack submarine and hovered in the water. Then, when they were ready, TJ gave them the signal to move off and they swam in single file behind him.

Bringing up the rear Mike was happy to follow the others through the murky green water. He was completely preoccupied with thoughts of dinner with Ali.

Mike lifted his glass and flashed a smile at the gorgeous woman sitting opposite him. "To Axe, his recovery and his match-making skills."

Ali touched her glass to his as their eyes locked. "To Axe."

Sipping his champagne, his gaze lingered on her. She wore a black, slim-fitting halter neck dress that showcased her elegant throat and ample cleavage. With her hair up and only enough makeup to emphasize her full lips and hazel eyes, she was stunning.

"I wanted to thank you for how much time you've spent with Axe. You've worked wonders for him… But, that's not why I invited you out to dinner."

She took a sip of champagne. "Really, then what's the reason?"

He leaned forward and whispered. "I'm trying to seduce you."

Eyes sparkling she pressed her lips together and swallowed. "Well it's working."

"Sir, your appetizer."

They both jumped at the waiter's voice.

Ali blushed as he placed their dishes in front of them and refilled their glasses.

"How did you find this place?" she asked once the waiter had left.

"A buddy of mine raved about it a few months back. I thought it was worth a try."

Ali finished a mouthful of the scallop. "Well, if the starter is anything to go on I think he was understating. If the meal is this good, I'm not going to have room for dessert."

"I know a great little café around the corner that serves an amazing pecan pie." He smiled suggestively. "They're open late."

She put on her best southern accent. "Why, Michael Saunders, you do know how to show a girl a good time."

As the lovebirds made eyes at each other another pair was watching them closely. Rick stood outside the French restaurant with a curvaceous blonde on his arm.

"Come on Ricky, you promised me dancing and a good time?"

"Damn it woman, give me a second." He could see that his boy Mike was completely smitten. He assumed that the pretty brunette was the veterinarian and it was clear that Romeo more than 'liked' her.

"Are you checking out that girl?" the blonde asked indignantly.

Rick scowled. "No, I only like hot pieces of ass like

you." He reached around and grabbed her buttocks. "Come on, let's get out of here."

As they walked down the street he sent a message to TJ.

Our boy is out to dinner with the vet and he's all loved up... Time for selection?

A moment later a reply hit his phone.

We'll get to the bottom of this tomorrow.

Chapter Eleven

Yawning, Mike dumped his gear bag on the bench in the team room and stretched his neck. He smiled to himself as he opened his locker and searched for a stick of deodorant. Last night was the most fun he'd had in months and all they'd done was talk.

He and Ali had left the restaurant at closing and continued flirting in a local café. They'd remained there till the early hours of the morning when the staff had forced them to leave. Only then, had Mike hailed her a cab then walked home.

He'd finally reached his apartment at four in the morning. Two hours was all the sleep he'd gotten before reporting for duty.

Rick entered the room. "Late night, brother?"

"Yeah, I could murder a cup of coffee."

"There's a pot in the briefing room. I'll grab one with you."

"Sounds good." Mike closed his locker and followed Rick into the lecture room they shared with the other squads. As he stepped through the doorway he spotted Ernie and TJ sitting side-by-side. Rick took the seat next to them. All three sat facing an empty chair.

He frowned. "Hey, what's up?"

"Take a seat, Mike." TJ nodded to the empty seat.

"What's this? Some kind of intervention?"

"You could call it that."

Mike turned the chair backward and straddled it. All of them, even Rick, sported stern expressions.

"Where were you last night?" TJ asked.

"Guys, seriously, what's this about?"

"Are you in love?" snapped Rick.

"Jesus, Rick, you couldn't interrogate a chimpanzee with a fist full of bananas," growled TJ.

Mike laughed. "So that's it?"

"You've been spending a lot of time with this Ali chick, brother," said TJ.

"Guys, she's been treating Axe. It's been kind of hard for me not to spend time with her. Why, is that a problem? You boys getting jealous?"

TJ shook his head. "Given your track record with women and relationships in general, we're concerned you're heading for another train wreck."

"Oh come on. I've only been on three dates with her."

TJ's eyes narrowed. "Rick, tell him."

"I saw you at the restaurant last night, Mike. I saw how you were looking at her. This is a bit more than a hit it and quit it."

Mike clenched his fists on his knees. "Fine, you got me. I really like this girl. There, I said it."

"Rick thinks you're head over heels in love with her," said TJ.

"He wouldn't know what love was if it punched him in the dick."

Rick let out a raucous burst of laughter. "Did I just get dissed on love by the guy whose last girlfriend was a psycho? Oh, and didn't the one before that steal all your shit when we were in Afghan?"

Mike scowled.

"This is for your own good," added TJ.

"What exactly is this?"

Ernie rocked back on his chair. "You remember, _essé_. The 'selection' course."

"Guys, that was a joke. You don't…"

All three men frowned.

"If she passes, we'll embrace her as one of our own," said TJ.

"But, if she fails," added Rick.

"Then she's out," finished Ernie.

Mike paused in thought. "Look, this girl isn't like the others. She's stable, compassionate and grounded. I don't think—"

TJ interrupted with a shake of his head. "Your track record suggests you don't think, slick. Trust me. This is for your own good."

Mike sighed. "OK, where do we start?"

"Tomorrow. It's Saturday. You're going to invite her on a hike with you up Mount Otay."

"What if she doesn't want to go?"

Rick laughed. "Then last night wasn't as special as you thought."

"So why the sudden urge to go hiking?" Ali asked as Mike pulled his truck into a parking lot at the base of a rugged mountain range.

"You mentioned you liked the outdoors and I thought it might be a good chance for us to get to know each other."

"Good idea, I like it." She pushed open the door and jumped out. "Come on. Let's do this."

Mike grabbed his backpack, locked the truck and led her through a camping ground to the trailhead.

As they climbed a narrow path up the side of a canyon, she turned to him. "Have you been up here before?"

"Once or twice."

"You bring all your girls up here?"

"No. Most of the women I've dated wouldn't climb into my truck much less a mountain."

"Really? Have you always dated princesses?"

Mike laughed. "Yeah, I guess I have. Let's just say you're nothing like them."

"I'm not exactly sure how to take that."

He smiled. "Trust me, it's a good thing. You're the best thing that's happened to me… and Axe, in a long time."

They reached the crest of the canyon and paused to take in the scenery. Mike dropped his pack on the ground and handed her a water bottle.

"You know, I could be a total princess. You'd have no way of knowing."

"That's what we're here to find out," said TJ over the covert communicator lodged inside Mike's ear.

Given the tiny device only had a range of a few hundred yards, he glanced around hoping to spot him. However, TJ was an experienced sniper and a master of camouflage, he wouldn't be seen.

Mike glanced at his watch. It was a little past midday.

"You OK to step it out? We'll make the peak in time for sunset and be back down before it gets too dark."

Smiling, Ali glanced back over her shoulder. "Sounds good." She held up the bottle of water. " You sure you don't want me to carry something other than this?"

"Nah, I'm good."

"Big strong SEAL and all that."

"Not at all. I'm just happy following your butt up the hill."

Mike's comment was rewarded by a puking sound in his ear. Clearly his flirting didn't impress TJ. Ali rolled her eyes and powered up the hill, leaving him in her dust. "OK, so that was cheesy," grunted Mike as he stepped off after her.

"No shit," added TJ over the radio.

It took them nearly three hours to climb to the peak of Mount Otay. When they finally reached the top they were greeted with a spectacular view across the Mexican border. Mike wiped the sweat from his brow as he dropped the heavy daypack on the ground. Ali had set a surprisingly fast pace up the mountain and, carrying the gear TJ had given him, Mike worked hard to keep up. His T-shirt was drenched in sweat and his legs were aching from the steep ascent.

"Wow. You can literally see for miles." She pointed at the spectacular vista stretched out before them. "That's Mexico, right?"

Pulling a fresh bottle of cold water from his pack he tossed it to her. "Right. I've gotta say, you're fitter than half the guys on team."

She snickered. "As if. But, do I pass the princess test?"

92

Mike raised an eyebrow. "What do you mean?"

"Come on." She shot him a cheeky smile, stepped closer to him, put her hands on his hips, and kissed his sweaty cheek. "It's pretty clear that you bought me up her to test my mettle. You're not looking for another princess, are you?"

"Not a chance." He covered her lips with his.

"You guys are making me sick."

This time it was Rick's voice that startled him, transmitting through the tiny radio lodged in his ear.

Mike made a point of prolonging the kiss for the observer's sake. When they finally broke, he scanned the terrain around them with a critical eye.

"What are you looking for?" asked Ali.

"Squirrels, sneaky squirrels."

Rick chuckled in his ear and whispered. "That's sneaky, secret, squirrel to you Romeo. And don't bother looking you ain't gonna find me, bro. I'm like a ghost."

"We need somewhere to set up our picnic and wait for sunset." He pointed to a rocky outcrop with a flat patch of sand in front of it. "How about over there?"

Mike hadn't had time to inspect the pack TJ had given him that morning. The Chief had assured him it contained everything he needed for a romantic hike. He took out a blanket and a cooler bag filled with a selection of cold meats, biscuits, fruits and cheeses.

As he offered her a cracker with a slice of cheddar, she whistled. "Wow, I'm impressed, sailor."

"So am I," he mumbled.

"OK Romeo, time to initiate phase two of the operation," said Rick in his ear. "I need you to excuse yourself for a trip to the little boy's room and head twenty yards down the hill, due east."

"Fine," he mouthed.

Ali was gazing at the horizon as she ate.

"Hey, babe, I've got to duck off to the little boy's room."

"You mean the little boy's boulder."

"Right," he said with a chuckle. Circling the outcrop, he started off into the scrub. After what he estimated was twenty yards, he stopped. "I'm here. Where are you?"

He nearly leaped out of his skin when a bush in front of him materialized into a figure. It was Rick, dressed in a shaggy sniper suit.

He grinned, revealing brilliant white teeth through the camouflage. "Hey, bro."

Mike shook his head. "Seriously, you guys are children."

"I know, isn't it awesome." A packet of *Starburst* appeared from under his camouflage and he offered one to Mike.

After the uphill climb, sugar was exactly what he needed. He took the candy, unwrapped it and chewed. "So, what the hell's TJ got planned now? I think Ali's proven she's no princess."

"Eh, so she climbed a hill. Let's see how she goes with sleeping rough on a mountain."

"Why in god's name would she do that?"

"Because you're going to feign an illness."

Mike shook his head. "She's a vet bud, which is a type of doctor. She'll see right through it."

"Not when you've got real symptoms."

He frowned. "Rick, what do you mean by symptoms?"

"You know, fever, stomach cramps, dizziness."

"And why would I have them?"

Rick grinned sheepishly. "Don't blame me, this one's on TJ."

Mike glanced at the *Starburst* wrapper he was rolling

between his fingers. His stomach gurgled. Suddenly he didn't feel well. "You sneaky motherfucker."

"Bro, it's for your own good."

"You're a dead man."

"Hey, at least this way you don't have to pretend, because pretending is lying, Mike. And that's bad."

"Mike, are you alright?" Ali called out from behind him.

He turned to see where she was. When he looked back, Rick was gone. "You guys have taken this too far."

"Don't worry. We'll be here watching over you like guardian angels, *essé*," transmitted Ernie, confirming that he was also part of the conspiracy.

"Hell's Angels more like it." As Mike ascended the slope he spotted Ali standing near the peak wearing a concerned expression.

"There you are."

As he got closer she frowned. "Mike, are you OK?"

His vision went blurry. He collapsed to his knees "No, I'm not feeling–" Projectile vomit spewed into the sand and he slumped to all fours. "Screw you, Rick."

The next half hour was a blur of throwing up and shivering as Rick's concoction played havoc with his intestines. Thankfully, Ali wasn't put off and helped him back to their picnic site where she propped him up against a rocky outcrop. She never left his side as she tried to get him to keep down water. After half an hour he was feeling slightly better but still couldn't stand. He wanted to curl into a ball and die.

"Mike, did you eat anything dubious in the last twenty-four hours?"

"Define dubious," he croaked.

"Seafood, dairy or chicken?"

"Um, all three." He managed to sit up and drink some of the water she offered him.

Ali found a medical kit in the backpack and handed him two aspirin. "This will help with your fever."

He took the pills before checking his watch. "It's getting late. I don't think I'm going to be able to get off the mountain before dark."

Ali wore a concerned expression as she glanced up from her phone. "Mike, I don't have any cell coverage. Do you?"

He managed to hand her his phone without vomiting.

She checked. "No bars. Do you want me to run down now and get help?"

He shook his head. "No. The path is treacherous and it'll be dark before you get halfway. Plus, I'm terrified of the dark, so there's no way you're leaving me here by myself."

Ali laughed. "Come on warrior, you're not afraid of coyotes and wolves are you?"

His eyes went wide. "You're shitting me. There are wolves out here?"

"Of course. I get at least one dog a week that's been badly mauled." She rose and started collecting dried branches from the surrounding bushes. "We'll make a fire. It'll keep them away."

He struggled to get to his feet and help. Another bout of dizziness and vomiting hit him.

"Hey, you need to rest up. If we have to spend the night here, that's fine. The temperature won't drop very far this time of year. Plus we've got a space blanket and plenty of water." Ali made a fist-sized pile of dried grass and placed the sticks she had collected next to it. "Do you have a lighter?"

Mike shook his head and groaned. "Is there one in the pack?"

"No."

He watched her open the medical kit and inspect the containers inside. "We do have potassium permanganate though." She continued rummaging through the kit. "If there's something with glycerin in it, we might be in business. Ah, huh. Jackpot!" She held up a bottle of hand sanitizer.

"What are you going to do with that?"

"Watch and learn." She opened a dressing and placed it on the ground. Then she tipped some of the potassium on it as well as a squirt of hand cleaner. Using a twig, she blended the two compounds. The mixture erupted into flame and she added kindling to it. In no time she had a small fire burning.

"Where did you learn that?"

"I went through a survival show phase. It was a bit of an addiction."

Mike's laugh turned to retching. "Seriously, I'm impressed, and a little bit emasculated."

"Hey, you rest up. When you're feeling better we'll walk out." She wandered a few yards from the fire to collect more branches. "Oh and who's Rick?" she asked over her shoulder. "When you were sick you kept abusing some guy called Rick."

"He's a buddy of mine. I'm pretty sure it's his cooking that did this to me."

"So we've got Rick to blame for a night out under the stars with you and the contents of your stomach."

"It would seem that way."

As the sun dipped below the horizon, Ali snuggled in next to him with the space blanket wrapped around their shoulders. With their little fire crackling in the cool evening air, they were actually very comfortable.

"It's so pretty out here," said Ali as the first stars appeared in the sky. "I don't think you should be so harsh on Rick."

"Yeah, we'll see about that." Mike slipped his arm around her back as he scanned the mountain landscape for any sign of his team-mates. "You're all in the shit," he mouthed.

"You're welcome," responded Rick from the darkness.

Mike subtly pried the device from his ear and buried it in the sand under him.

"You OK?"

"Yeah, I had a bug in my ear."

"You're not having a great time up here, are you tiger?" She passed him a bottle of water.

He rinsed his mouth. "It's not that bad. I've got you here with me."

She patted his cheek. "You're so sweet when you're not puking all over the place."

"Oh, you had to bring that up."

Ali laughed. "I see what you did there."

"I'm sorry, it just came out."

She snorted. "Right, no more. Topic change, how many kids do you want?"

"Wow, trap a man on a mountain and hit him with the big ones."

"That's right, handsome. You're a captive audience."

"Well, I definitely want kids. But not while I'm still in the SEALs. I'm not missing out on them growing up, like my dad did."

"You said he was Navy?"

"Yeah, I didn't get to see much of him." Mike took

another sip of water. "Don't get me wrong, he was a great father, when he was around."

"Is he still alive?"

"No, cancer got him." He handed the bottle to her. "What about you? Want kids?"

"Three, a boy and two girls."

"You've got all this worked out, haven't you?"

"It's a girl thing."

They sat silently gazing out over the mountains. The stars shone brightly in a cloudless sky, the lights of Tijuana sparkling along the coast.

"You sure you didn't plan this?" she asked, snuggling into him.

He was thankful the darkness hid his face. "No, why would you ask that?"

"Because this is about as romantic as it gets."

Chapter Twelve

The squad was already assembled in the briefing room when Mike finally arrived at work. In the corner of the room, stood a whiteboard with his name on one side and Ali's on the other. Under her name they'd written a list of attributes: flexible, endurance, problem solving, nurturing, not a princess.

Under his name they'd written a single phrase: pukey whiner.

Rick was the first to spot him. "Morning, Bear Grylls, how'd you sleep?"

His lip lifted in a snarl. "You know exactly how I slept, douche bag."

Ernie snickered. "Looked pretty cozy, all snuggled up with your princess charming."

"Yeah, she rode in on her big white horse and saved your ass," added Rick.

"You guys are bastards. I'm going to pay you back for this, and when I do–"

"Hey, Romeo," interrupted TJ. "There's no harm done.

In fact, not only have we tested the mettle of your future wife, but we also brought you two closer. The crucible of adversity has forged a bond between you that will not easily be broken. What more could you want?"

Mike, Rick and Ernie all stared at the craggy Chief in silence.

"What the fuck, TJ. Have you been reading some Tony Robins shit or something?" asked Rick.

Mike sighed. "As much as I hate to say it, he's right. Last night Ali really came through for me."

"Steady on, brother. She's through the first gateway, but we're a long way from bashing a trident on her chest," said TJ.

Mike slumped into a chair. "What's next then?"

"A subject close to my heart," said Rick.

"Let me guess; some kind of gold digger test?"

"Correct."

TJ flipped over the whiteboard to reveal a detailed list of actions and reactions. "Listen up, whelps, this is how it's going down."

Mike held up his hand. "Stop. Can I please have one night off to take her out for dinner? You put her through hell, and she deserves a break."

"You sure she's the one who needs a break?" asked Rick.

Mike glared at him.

TJ turned to Ernie, who nodded. "OK, tonight the GSC is on hold. But the day after, we're back on schedule."

Mike nodded. Small wins were all that he was going to get at this stage.

"Where you going to take her?" asked TJ.

He shrugged. "I haven't thought that far ahead."

The Chief fixed him with a stare. "You like this girl, right?"

"Um, yeah."

"OK, an old buddy of mine owns a pretty good restaurant over in Little Italy. It's called Just 'n' Thyme. I'll give him a call and get you a table. He's also got shares in the Old Ken cinema. Take the girl to see something nice."

Mike was a little taken back. TJ had just dropped the name of one of the most exclusive restaurants in the city. He knew that because Stacey had wanted to go, but they'd been booked solid for six weeks. "Thanks, TJ."

"No problems." The veteran SEAL cracked his knuckles. "OK, so back to the plan. Mike, tomorrow night you're going to cook for her, and then take the following day off."

Mike's eyes narrowed. "There has to be a catch."

TJ grinned. "It's a selection course. Hell yeah, there's a catch."

As TJ briefed the squad on the next phase of the Girlfriend Selection Course the subject of their planning was chatting with her sister in the veterinary clinic's waiting room.

Leonie handed over a large coffee. "So, what the hell happened last night?"

"You're an angel." Ali took a sip. "Where do I start?

"At the beginning." Leonie took a seat.

"So, Mike took me on a hike up Mount Otay."

Her sister grimaced. "Really, that sounds about as romantic as dinner with Donald Trump."

"No. Actually, it was amazing. He packed a lovely picnic. The view was beautiful."

Leonie's eyebrows rose. "And let me guess, you stayed on the mountain all night making love under the stars."

"Not exactly."

"Oh god, what happened?"

She sighed. "Mike got hit with a bad bout of food poisoning. He was vomiting and dizzy, the works. We had to spend the night out in the wilderness."

"What a nightmare."

"Not at all, it was kind of nice. I lit a fire and we talked until he fell asleep. By morning everything was fine."

"So, you nursed him all night. What can I say. Honey, you're a sucker for a wounded critter."

"I got the feeling that the whole climbing the mountain thing was a bit of a test."

Her sister grinned. "And you passed it with flying colors. So what's next? When are you going to see this super stud again?"

"Well…" Her eyes sparkled. "Tonight, he's taking me out to apologize for the mountain fiasco."

"Oooh, where you going?"

"Just 'n' Thyme."

"Get out of town. How'd he get a booking at such short notice?"

She shrugged. "I have no idea. Then we're going to a rom-com at the Ken Cinema."

"Girl, this boy is pulling out all the stops. You're going to get yourself some sweet loving tonight, and I want all the juicy details."

"You're incorrigible." She took another sip of the coffee. "Now, what's going on with you? How did the girl's camp go?"

Leonie groaned. "Let's not talk about that. Tell me all the details of this new man. I bet he's got a massive…" She wiggled her finger suggestively.

Ali snorted into her coffee, dribbling it down the front of her scrubs. "Leonie, I haven't slept with him."

"Yeah, but I bet you've felt it through his jeans all thick and throbbing."

"Leonie, we're not having this conversation."

"Oh, we just did baby. That one's going straight in the double click bin."

"The what?"

"You know. The place I store mental images for when I double click the mouse."

She raised her hand. "Enough. I love you sis but that's too much information."

"Not at all. By the way, I'll be here tomorrow for all the juicy details."

"I won't be here. I'm taking the day off and, Mike is too."

"Ooh, a lazy day of sex… that's even better."

Standing she kissed her sister on the cheek. "Get the hell out of here. I've got work to do."

"Is that how you order your SEAL around?"

"Out!"

"Fine, I'm going. But tomorrow, I want all the details."

Chapter Thirteen

Mike wrapped his arm around Ali's shoulders as they left the Ken Cinema and walked the dark streets of the city. Despite the late hour she felt safe nestled against her SEAL. "What did you think of the movie?"

She felt him shrug.

"Ah… It was good."

"The truth please."

He chuckled. "OK, I thought it was a little cheesy."

Ali laughed. "It's a rom-com. What did you expect from Sandra Bullock and Ryan Reynolds? It's meant to be cheesy. That's the point."

Mike dropped his hand to her waist. "I have to admit, I've always liked Sandra Bullock."

She smiled. "Oh, really. Here's me thinking you're more of a Reece Witherspoon kind of guy."

"No way, Bullock is sassy and seriously sexy. I've seen everything she's in."

"Me too. Which one's your favorite?"

"You mean, apart from the Proposal?" He winked. "I loved her in Miss Congeniality."

"You're kidding?"

"Nope, I really like that movie."

She snuggled in against his arm. "Me too. I must have watched it at least fifty times."

"Let's dig it out on a rainy day," said Mike as they turned into a park and walked along a gravel path. "Although I'm not watching the sequel, it was crap."

"Yes it was."

"Ali, I hope tonight's made up for the debacle on the mountain."

"Are you kidding? It's been perfect. I've never had the chef hand deliver his signature dish before."

"And I'm sure he's never had someone ask to take the bones home in a doggy bag."

She shot him a frown. "I bet he's never met a dog like Axe either."

Stopping, he stepped in front of her, ducked his head and kissed her. "And that's why Axe… loves you."

"Just Axe?" she murmured.

As he kissed her again he expected to feel panic at her words… but he didn't. He'd never been with a woman who made him feel so elated yet at the same time content. It was the piece that had been missing in all his relationships. "He's had more time with you."

She smiled. "This is true."

As they continued along the path Mike reflected on the date. TJ's contact had pulled out all the stops for them. If he didn't know better he'd suspect that the Chief was setting him up for some kind of test.

Pausing, Mike scanned the park ahead of them. His eyes

darted across the dim landscape. He could see a jogger in the distance and someone walking a dog. Nothing that suggested trouble, and yet he couldn't shrug off the feeling that something wasn't quite right.

"You OK?"

His eyes snapped back to her. "Hey, yeah I'm good." Almost instantly the feeling of uneasiness was replaced with something else. Exhaling softly, he took a moment to appreciate her beauty. Her eyes shone in the soft glow cast from the park's lights. Tipping his head, he pressed his lips against hers and wrapped his arms around her waist. She responded eagerly and seconds turned into minutes as they embraced.

"Hey, pal."

The voice was slurred.

Mike spun toward the figure approaching them and stepped protectively in front of Ali. "How can I help you?"

"You can give me your wallet, asshole," the man hissed, pulling a knife from under his grubby jacket.

Ali gasped.

Mike quickly assessed their assailant. His hair and beard were matted, his eyes bloodshot. The stench of body odor filled the air as he approached. When he wasn't talking his jaw was clenched and grinding. "Let's not do anything stupid."

"Listen, punk," the mugger slurred.

Mike sprung into action. One hand clamped down on the wrist of the knife hand, the other further up the arm. Wrenching the man's wrist backward he forced him to his knees. The knife clattered on the sidewalk and he kicked it clear.

"Stop, it hurts," he wailed as Mike forced him onto his

stomach and locked his arm behind him. Only then did he check on Ali. "You OK?"

She stared at him with wide eyes. "Yeah, yeah I'm fine."

"Can you call 9-1-1?"

She fumbled with her purse. "Of course."

A patrol car responded in a matter of minutes and in no time the perp was cuffed and detained inside. Mike gave the officer a statement before they continued their walk.

"I'm really sorry you had to see that," said Mike softly.

Ali stopped, grabbed his face and kissed him. "You're amazing. I feel so safe when I'm with you and now I know why."

They broke and he smiled. "No, you're amazing and I've got a dog that can walk now to prove it."

"Shall we go see him?"

"It's your night, babe. I thought you might like to grab some gelato for dessert."

Her teeth flashed, a cheeky grin. "I've got some in my freezer."

"Sounds good."

Mike glanced over his shoulder as they left the park. He couldn't shake the feeling they were still in danger.

Ali lived in a quiet, semi-rural suburb on the outskirts of San Diego. It was a short drive from the clinic where they'd stopped to feed Axe the remains of Ali's T-bone. Then, bidding goodnight to the dog, they had driven to her townhouse.

As Mike killed the engine, she faced him smiling. "Thanks for a wonderful evening."

"An absolute pleasure." He leaned across and planted a long kiss on her. Lifting his head, he said, "Let me get your door."

As he made his way around to her side of the truck, Ali smiled to herself. Say what you would about military guys, but they were gentlemen. Or at least Mike was. One look at her tight dress and heels and he had taken it upon himself to lift her in and out of the truck. That was fine with her. His hands on her waist and the scent of his cologne sent her heart racing, every time.

A moment later he opened the door. "Here you are, little lady."

She stepped onto the running board and kissed him again as he wrapped his hands around her waist. He was hard against her as they pashed. Leonie was right, she could feel how large he was.

"I think we should take this inside," she managed between bouts of passion.

He cupped her buttocks. "You sure?"

"Yes, I'm sure." She moaned as he lifted her out of the truck. Pushing the cab door closed he carried her across the lawn to the porch. Somehow, between kisses, she found her keys and he unlocked the front door. "Where to?"

"Second room on the right."

He swept down the hall into the master bedroom. As he lowered her gently onto the bed he kicked off his loafers. In the soft light from the street lamps outside her window she caught his cheeky smile.

"What?"

"Damn you're sexy."

She moaned as he lowered himself on to her, his lips traced her ear lobe and she shuddered with delight. All thoughts of playing hard to get were out the window as she unbuttoned his shirt.

"So, we're not going to take this slow?"

"Are you kidding me?" Her voice was husky. "I've wanted your hands on me all night."

"I've made a good impression then?"

She managed to completely undo his shirt exposing his chiseled abdomen. "You could say that."

Mike slid his hand under her dress and ran it up her leg to her waist as he kissed her. His touch was electric. She arched her back as his hand slid to her inner thigh.

"I want you now," she gasped as he redirected his attention back to the lobe of her ear.

"I've wanted you since we first kissed."

His warm breath sent her into overdrive. "Not before then?"

"OK, maybe when you hit that first bullseye." He bunched her dress up on both sides of her hips and slid it over her head. Kissing her neck, he unsnapped her bra and freed her breasts.

She bit her lip as his mouth found her nipple and he took it gently between his teeth. His hands roamed her body, stoking the fire that burned inside. "Promise me I'm not just another notch on your belt," she said as he kissed her neck.

He paused. "I like you, Ali, I like you a lot."

Her full lips formed a smile. "Then why are your clothes still on?"

Mike slid off the bed and out of his pants in one smooth maneuver. Noticing that the curtains were open he reached across to close them. Glancing out the window he spotted a white sedan parked across the street.

Ali let out a sigh. "Are you teasing me on purpose or just giving my neighbors something to look at?"

Mike pushed the car from his mind as he turned. Laughing, he climbed onto the bed and lowered himself on top of her.

She gazed up at him with lustful eyes. "I hope you weren't planning on sleeping tonight."

Chapter Fourteen

Mike slipped through the door to the briefing room. The unit's intelligence officer had already begun his presentation to the platoon. Ducking into the back row he took a seat next to Rick.

"Where you been?" whispered Rick. "TJ ain't happy you weren't in for the run this morning."

"I slept in. What have I missed?"

Rick's brow shot up. "You slept in?"

"Yeah."

Grinning, Rick lifted his hand. "High-five, brother."

Mike left him hanging. "Anything new on the Butcher?"

"Nope. He's gone to ground."

"Damn."

At the front of the room the intelligence officer paused and advanced his slides. "That concludes the latest target updates. What I'm going on with now is the assessment from Homeland Security."

"This ought to be good," mumbled Rick.

Among the SEALs, Homeland Security had a reputation for releasing alarmist reporting that they usually ignored.

"The latest assessment indicates that, due to recent successes against the Mexican cartels, there may be an increased threat to military personnel in the San Diego area. Although the Butcher has gone to ground, Homeland thinks he might be looking to conduct a revenge attack stateside. Team Five has been identified as a potential target."

One of the SEALs thrust his hand in the air. "Hey, sir."

"What's up, Dean?"

"If Barbosa wants revenge won't that make him easier to target. I mean he's got to coordinate that shit, right?"

"True, but it also means we need to be vigilant. Guys, you need to report any suspect behavior. When off base make sure you maintain a low profile. That means no military style training shirts, no Oakleys and no cargo pants. Remind your wives that dressing kids in cammo or SEAL branding is a bad idea."

Rick lifted his hand. "What about Team Five limited edition assless chaps. Is Mike still allowed to wear them?"

The officer chuckled. "Rick, what you and Mike wear in the Blue Oyster is completely up to you. OK, if there's no other questions, we're done here."

As the SEAL operators filed out of the room TJ rose and made eye contact with each of the squad. "Alpha, we're staying." He waited till they were alone. "Mike, good of you to join us."

Rick slapped Mike on the shoulder. "He slept in."

He shook his head. "Thanks, bud."

"Well, I hope you're all rested up because we're moving into the final phase of the selection course."

Mike sighed. "Come on guys, Ali—"

"Still hasn't passed," shot Rick. "Bro, you made a promise. You gonna break a promise to your team-mates?"

He shook his head.

TJ fixed him with a steely gaze. "Good, because tonight is stir-Friday."

"Except it's Thursday, *esse*," corrected Ernie.

"Yeah, it's a joke," said TJ.

Ernie snorted. "Not funny, you shouldn't tell jokes, Chief."

"You know what is funny?" TJ said. "Beach running in waterlogged dive masks."

"OK, I take it back. It's funny."

"I thought as much. Alright, tonight Mike is going to cook for the lady."

"Yeah, we went through it yesterday, I've got it," said Mike. "I make the pasta and you guys run the mission. Look, this might be nothing but I keep seeing the same white sedan around town."

TJ frowned. "You think it might be related to the Homeland assessment?"

Mike shrugged. "It could be nothing."

"It could be something, you get plates?"

"Negative, there wasn't one on the back. I haven't seen it from the front."

"Well, let's keep an eye out and if it turns up again we'll check it out."

Later that evening, only a few miles from Coronado, Ali arrived at Mike's fifth floor apartment. He gave her a quick tour, before returning to the preparation of their dinner. It was pretty much exactly as Ali expected a military guy's place to look. Sleek, clean and with the exception of a few photos, completely devoid of personal effects. With a glass of wine in hand, she checked out the balcony and the view. Even at night it was spectacular. She could see all the way out across the parklands to the USS Midway museum.

"Great place and a killer view," she said, reentering the apartment.

Mike turned from the stove. "Thanks, I don't get to spend as much time here as I'd like. Although, I'm thinking I'll have to move. Once Axe is better he's going to need a yard."

Leaning against the bench top she watched him chop fresh parsley. "They won't let him go back to work?"

The knife paused, mid-slice. "Do you think he'll be physically able?"

"In time, yes. He's made great progress in the last week."

"That would be awesome. However, I'd need the Army vet to retract his original assessment."

"I could definitely help with that. I can be very persuasive when I need to be."

Mike rinsed his hands in the sink and dried them on his apron before leaning across the counter and kissing her. "Don't I know it."

"So what exactly are you cooking?" she asked as he returned to preparing food.

He dipped a wooden spoon into the pot and tasted the contents. It's an Italian dish that my mom taught me to make. I hope you like pasta."

"Love it." She watched him open the oven, letting steam escape into the room. The rich smells of chocolate and whiskey flooded her nostrils. "Oh, my god, what is that smell?"

"That's the *piece de resistance*. My mom's Mississippi mud cake. It's a secret family recipe." Taking a baking tin from the oven he placed it on the bench top and draped it with a clean dishcloth. "Now, all that's left is to cook the pasta and we're in business. I hope you're hungry."

Ali slid around the granite island and stood behind him as he reached into an overhead cupboard. "Yeah, about that." She kissed the back of his neck and slipped her hands around to his hard stomach. "I was kind of hoping we could take a few minutes to work up an appetite."

Mike abandoned his search for the pasta. Turning his head, he muttered against her lips, "That sounds like a good idea."

As she pressed her breasts against his back, her fingers slid beneath the waistband of his jeans. "I thought you might like it."

He moaned as he tensed against her. Then, turning, he scooped her off the ground so she was straddling him. They kissed as he sat her on the bench and she wrapped her legs around him. "You have all the best ideas," he managed, sliding off her T-shirt.

Her jeans followed a moment later, tossed into the corner of the kitchen.

"You better turn off that sauce or it's going to burn," panted Ali.

He reached out and flicked the cooktop off. "We can always eat cake."

"Sex and cake? You're possibly the sexiest man I've ever met." She ripped off his shirt as he dropped his pants.

"Yeah, well I'm not letting you leave. For the next twenty-four hours you're mine."

Ali relaxed in a deck chair on Mike's balcony, enjoying her coffee and a bowl of cereal. She and Mike had spent the morning in bed. He'd made breakfast, then dashed out for a run while she took the opportunity to check her emails and grab some sun.

A thump on the door startled her. She shrugged a bathrobe on over her underwear and walked across the apartment. "Who is it?"

"Delivery for a Michael Saunders."

She opened the door, but left the security chain in place.

The man on the other side stuffed a letter through the gap. "Where's Mister Saunders?" he demanded.

Ali could see the guy was big and middle aged. She put him in his late forties, possibly fifties. He had gray hair, a weathered face and intense gray eyes.

"Can I take a message?"

"So he lives here. Good. Give him this letter and tell him this is a courtesy call. If he doesn't pay up, we're going to take his truck."

She took the letter.

"You understand?"

"Yes." She closed the door and slid the bolt shut. Examining the letter, she walked across to the bench where she had previously spotted a pile of mail. As she added the envelope to the heap she noticed that most of the open documents in the pile were overdue bills. It looked as if Mike was in financial trouble.

She returned to the balcony and was about to sit when there was another knock at the door. "Are you serious?" she murmured.

"Mike, Mike, I know you're in there!" a female's high-pitched voice yelled.

Ali frowned. Who was this woman and what the hell was she doing at Mike's door at eleven o'clock on a Wednesday morning?

"Mike, you can change your number but I know you haven't moved!" she screamed. "Baby, come on, let me in. I know you're there. I know we can work this out."

Ali padded quietly across to the door and looked through the security peephole. The woman outside was pretty, very pretty in fact. Her hair was honey blonde and her lips a slash of bright red lipstick. Vision through the hole was limited, but she could make out a black singlet and what she hoped were fake boobs. Mike wasn't kidding when he said Ali wasn't like any of his ex's.

"I bet you didn't make it up Mount Otay, did you sweetheart?" she whispered.

"Fine, you know what, fuck you, Mike. I was the best thing that ever happened to you and you completely screwed it. You chose that stupid dog over me. Now you can sleep alone at night."

Ali tried not to laugh as the woman stomped off in her high heels. "So that's the infamous Stacey." Mike had told her about the ex and what had happened after Axe had been shot. One thing was for sure; Ali would never make him choose between her and the dog. Axe had saved Mike's life. For that reason alone she would never begrudge his feelings for the dog. However, the whole issue with his finances was something that concerned her.

She pondered the issue for half an hour before the sound of a key in the lock signaled his return.

Shirtless and coated with sweat, he bent and kissed her. "Hey, you."

Ali exhaled as she drank in his lean muscular frame.

"I'm going to grab a shower. You want in?" he asked dropping his shorts and standing naked in the living room.

She rose, letting the bathrobe slide off her body revealing her underwear. Unclipping her bra, she released her breasts and stood with her hands on her hips and watched him grow. Their talk about his finances could wait.

An hour later, still damp from the shower, Mike prepared a chicken salad. He served it with a slice of mud cake, drenched in cream.

"So, your ex dropped by while you were out."

He stopped slicing tomatoes and turned to her, with a scowl. "Stacey? What did she want?"

"I think she was trying to make amends. I didn't let her in. She's got quite the potty mouth."

"I'm so sorry you had to experience that."

"Kind of reflects poorly on you, Michael."

He looked up from tossing the salad. "How do you mean?"

"Well, she definitely wouldn't have made it up the mountain, so clearly you were thinking with your dick not your brain. You've got to tighten up your testing process, Mike."

He swallowed nervously as he placed bowls on the island. "Testing process. I'm not sure I know what you mean?" Head bent, he returned to the salad.

"Babe, are you OK?" she asked.

"Huh, sorry no, I'm just a little preoccupied with something."

"Do you want to talk about it?"

"No, it's nothing for you to worry about."

She sighed. "Look, Mike. You had another visitor. A debt collector who told me to give you this." She reached for the letter from the pile next to her. "He said if you don't pay they'll take your truck. If you're having financial problems, Mike, you can talk to me about it."

His jaw clenched as he read the letter. "It's nothing I can't handle. Got a little behind on a few things because I was away. I'll get them sorted this week." Scrunching the note into a ball, he tossed it in the sink.

"Alright. But if you need a hand, just let me know. I'd be happy to waive all of Axe's medical costs."

He turned to face her. "You'd do that for me?"

She nodded. "You're a good guy Mike and–"

"Go on."

"And, I more than like you."

He wiped his hands on a dishcloth. "Why haven't I ever met a woman like you before?" he asked, rounding the counter.

She arched an eyebrow and shot him a smile. "We covered that."

Mike wrapped his arms around her waist and kissed her gently. Her mouth met his eagerly and the kiss gained intensity as his hands caressed her. "You're the most amazing woman I've ever met," he whispered breathlessly.

───────────

Ali sat on a park bench with her sister watching her nieces playing in a sandbox. The toddlers hadn't spotted her yet. They were completely enthralled with the plastic spades and buckets that she'd previously bought them.

Stretching her neck, Leonie enjoyed the escape. "So give me the sordid details."

Ali shook her head. "The sex is great and that's all you're getting."

Her sister feigned horror. "Oh, come on. You've got to give me more than that. Seriously, do you know the last time Steve and I had sex? I can't remember the last time he got up close and personal with my vagina."

Ali grimaced. "T.M.I."

"Come on, don't be a bitch, Ali."

She laughed. "Enough. Fine, all I'm going to say is that it's the best sex I've ever had. His body, god, it's carved from granite. He seriously looks like an artist sculpted him. And yet, he's so gentle, caring and considerate. He literally satisfies my every need."

"And his..." Leonie wiggled her finger.

She smiled. "More than adequate."

"God, I knew it. You're such a lucky bitch. Now, whatever you do don't have kids with him. It'll wreck everything. I'm serious. Before we had the devil spawn, we used to bang every five minutes. Steve was a demon. He took me in the kitchen, the bathroom, the laundry, it didn't matter. He just wanted me twenty-four seven—"

One of the girls screamed, interrupting her tirade. The youngest had grabbed a fist full of her sister's hair and was yanking it.

Leonie rose from the bench. "And then, these little angels arrived."

Ali watched as her sister untangled the girls and kissed each on the cheek. She smiled to herself as she reflected on what a great father Mike would make. He was patient, kind and gentle. The way he treated Axe also proved he was compassionate. However, his underlying financial issues were concerning.

"Hey, lover girl. What's on your mind?"

"Huh, nothing."

"Come on. We don't keep secrets from each other. What's up?"

"It's Mike, he's got himself in some financial trouble. Forgot to pay some bills when he was away on a mission."

"How much trouble?"

"I'm not sure. A debt collector came to his apartment this morning and told me they were going to take his truck."

"You're kidding me. Ali, that's a bit of a red flag. Surely a Navy SEAL can sort out his finances?"

"I know. The problem is I think I'm falling for him. He's so gentle and thoughtful, Leonie. He's a gentleman, an amazing lover and he even cooks. You know he disarmed a mugger the other night?"

"Oh shit, the full package."

"Yeah. But it isn't all smooth sailing. Since I started seeing him I feel like I'm constantly being challenged. First there was the mountain climb and the night of sickness and now this. It's as if the universe is conspiring against us."

"Look, Ali. If there's one piece of advice I can give you it's to follow your heart. There were plenty of things that got in the way of Steve and I. But we still made it through and now look at us. Two beautiful terrors... and no sex."

Ali wrapped her arms around her sister. "I know I don't say this enough, but I love you so much."

"Me too, bubs. I just want to see you happy. So, SEAL or no SEAL, if this guy breaks your heart I'm going to break his perfectly sculpted legs."

"Well, if it makes you feel better we're going to one of

his team-mates for dinner tomorrow night and they've got two little boys. Mike says they're horrendous."

"Oh, joy. What's that? Date number five and the most romantic of all. Dinner with hyperactive midgets."

"At least, he's introducing me to his friends. That's got to be a good sign, right?"

"Definitely. Military guys take introductions to their buddies very seriously. But, if you have to drop your keys in a bowl on the way in, run like hell. But first, text me the address."

Ali punched her gently in the shoulder. "You and your one-track mind."

Ramirez was the only spectator at the training session. He watched as his son intercepted the soccer ball and dribbled it toward the goal. "Go Carlos!" he screamed as the boy lined up and kicked. The ball went wide, hitting the side post, and ricocheted off across the boundary.

"Good try, son," he shouted encouragingly as the boy, shoulders slumped, trotted toward him. "It is better to try and miss, than never try at all."

The boy shook his head and joined the back of the lineup as another child attempted the drill.

Ramirez's phone vibrated. He pulled it from his jacket. "Hello."

"When are you going to kill the fucking SEAL?"

He coolly held the phone away from his ear until the Butcher's tirade was finished. Then he brought it closer and spoke. "Many of the pieces are already in place. I am waiting on the last of my men to have the necessary documentation and then we will move."

"I want it done as soon as possible."

"These things are better not rushed. They require meticulous planning and rehearsals to ensure they are successful."

"Do you remember what happened to the last man who failed me?"

Ramirez paused. "I've never failed you before, why would I now? You forget who I am, Vicente Barbosa. I am the man that people go to when they want the impossible done. I am the man who can kill anyone… for the right price. I'm not a man you want to threaten."

Barbosa fell silent for a full ten seconds. "I have never given you a task more important than this. My family's honor is at stake. When you are successful, I will double your fee."

"Your kindness is appreciated. If things go according to plan, in forty-eight hours you will have your revenge."

"I want to see the pain on his face as he watches his woman die. Then, bring me his head."

"It can be arranged so you can watch."

"The Americans are trying to capture me. I cannot leave Mexico."

"You will not have to leave the safety of your home. Their deaths will be broadcast over the internet to your computer, for a nominal fee."

"Excellent, I look forward to the show."

"I will make the necessary arrangements." He terminated the call and turned his attention back to his son's soccer training.

His wife approached with a drink in each hand. "Was that work?"

"Yes."

"And?"

He turned to her, unable to hide his grim expression. "I'm sorry, but I'm afraid I can't make the game on Sunday."

She shook her head and turned away.

Ramirez fought the urge to curse. Instead he focused his attention on his phone. If he was going to be sleeping on the couch, then he may as well spend the night with his mistress.

Chapter Fifteen

Mike stood outside a three-story brick structure stenciled with the letters MOE. The Method of Entry building's many walls were adorned with every type of window or doorway that the SEALs were likely to encounter. The teams spent hours perfecting the art of bashing, chopping, cutting, and blowing their way into the building. Then, overnight, a team of maintenance staff would return it to its original condition, so they could attack it again.

TJ and the rest of the squad were in one of the explosives preparation bays, hidden behind a bank of dirt. Not wanting to talk to them, Mike had volunteered to set up the house. Seething he lifted a wooden door and made to slot it into its retaining brackets. TJ and the others had made him look like an idiot to Ali. He'd never borrowed a dime in his life, paying cash for his truck and everything in his apartment. Not to mention, Ali didn't have a gold digging bone in her body. The door failed to slide into the bracket and he gave it a solid kick.

TJ appeared holding a breaching charge attached to an extendable pole. "You all good?"

He managed to shove the door in place. "No, I'm not good." He spun and spotted Ernie and Rick joining them. "Which one of you assholes dumped the late notices at my place?" The sheepish look on Rick's face confirmed his suspicions. "I want my spare key back. None of you assholes can be trusted."

There was an awkward silence, then TJ spoke, "So, how was your day off?"

"Apart from Ali thinking I'm an idiot?" He paused. "Yeah, good I guess. I hope you enjoyed your little repo man cameo."

"I was pretty convincing, yeah. Although I'm surprised she hasn't dumped you."

"Why would she?"

Ernie laughed. "Because you're broke, holmes."

"Well I ain't saying she's a gold digga, but she ain't messing with a broke nigga," added Rick.

"Did you seriously just quote Kanye?"

Rick grinned. "You know I did, brother."

"You're enjoying this, aren't you," snapped Mike. "You're putting this woman through hell and you're enjoying it. You're all enjoying it." Their silence confirmed his assessment. "I thought as much."

All three men broke into righteous laughter.

"Come on, bud. Remember this is for your own good. And I gotta say, so far this girl is kicking selection in the butt," said Rick.

"We'll see," grumbled TJ. "Yeah, so far so good, but this next phase is the moneymaker." He held up his explosive charge. "Let's test this bang."

"Hang on, what do you mean by another phase?" Mike asked over his shoulder as he grabbed his helmet and eye protection. He joined the Chief at the door he'd installed. "She's been through enough. I think she's proven her mettle."

TJ pressed himself against the wall with the pole at arm's length, the charge resting against the door. "Not yet she hasn't. Eyes and ears, take cover!"

Mike checked his gear and tucked in behind TJ. "Ready."

Ernie and Rick did the same.

"How many more phases are there?"

TJ held up two fingers. "Fire in the hole."

A deafening explosion shook the building, covering them in dust and smoke.

"So, what are the final phases?"

"You already know the next one, *essé*," said Ernie as they inspected the door.

The charge had split it neatly in two, throwing both halves inside.

"I'd call that a clean breach," said TJ.

"I don't know what the hell you're talking about, Ernie."

"Family, bro, it's all about family."

TJ nodded. "Damn straight it is, Ernie. Behind every SEAL there should be a strong wife, capable of running the household in his absence."

"Yeah, and you don't get a household crazier than this motherfucker's." Rick gestured to his offsider.

Mike shook his head. "Oh shit, you're not going to…"

Ernie slapped him on the shoulder. "Hell yeah we are, frogman. Dinner. My place. Seventeen hundred. Make sure she doesn't wear anything real nice. The boys have taken to throwing poop."

"You're shitting me?"

"Oh, they'll shit you alright." Rick grinned. "From head to toe."

"So, you work with Ernie, right?" Ali asked, as Mike pulled his truck into the driveway of the Ernesto residence. Located a few miles from the San Diego River, the home was a large single-story, stucco hacienda painted white with a red tiled roof. The front garden was tastefully landscaped as a desert setting, complete with cacti and red boulders.

"Correct, he's in my squad. His wife, Maria, is probably the best Mexican cook in San Diego."

"And, they've got two boys that are out of control?"

"Yeah, but don't mention that to Maria. She thinks they're total angels."

"Most mothers do."

He knocked on the door. A moment later it opened and Ernie greeted them with a broad smile, welcoming them inside. Maria, a pint-sized brunette with a huge bosom, appeared from the kitchen and embraced him in a bear hug. "Mike, how's that beautiful dog of yours doing?"

"Great, thanks to the skills of this amazing woman. Maria, this is Alison."

"Oh, the new girl. Ernie has told me a lot about you. So you're the one who's finally managed to rope my adopted son?"

Mike shot Ernie a questioning look.

"She doesn't know," he mouthed back.

"I don't know about roping him." Ali laughed.

"Well, you're the only one he's ever brought around here, so that makes you pretty special. Now, excuse me, I've got to finish preparing dinner. Ernie, get them a drink and take Ali out back to meet the boys."

"Yes, Maria."

A moment later, with ice-cold *Pacificos* in hand, they walked outside onto a wide deck overlooking a beautiful garden.

"Looking good, brother," said Mike as he surveyed the lush green lawn.

"Thanks, finally got it finished last week."

Ali spotted the boys playing in the sandbox under their stilted cubby house. A few feet away, on the grass, a Border Collie watched them intently.

"James, Ryan, come and say hello to our guests," called Ernie.

The two boys crawled out of the sandbox and trundled across the grass toward them. Dressed in matching sets of coveralls, Ali put their age at around four and five. They were adorable and resembled their parents, with dark hair, brown eyes and olive skin.

"Hey, guys," said Mike as they ran toward him and latched on to his legs.

"Mike, where's Axe?" one of the boys asked.

"He's not feeling great at the moment, Ryan. When he's better I'll bring him around."

"Who's that?" asked the younger of the two, James. He hid behind Mike's legs, peeking around at Ali.

"Oh my god, they're so cute," she said.

"This is Doctor Ali, she's helping Axe to get better," said Mike.

"Is that your girlfriend?" asked Ryan. "Mom says you can't find a good girlfriend."

Mike reached down, grabbed him by the coveralls and tossed him over his shoulder. "Is that right? Well your mom wouldn't know, because she's too busy bossing your dad around." The boy squealed with delight.

"Michael Saunders, I heard that." Maria was standing in the doorway to the living area with her hands on her hips.

"You're in trouble," sang James as he clapped.

Mike lowered Ryan to the ground and grinned sheepishly. "Every man wants a strong woman, Maria."

"Dinner is served," she growled.

"Dad loves it when Mike comes around," said Ryan as they walked inside.

"Why is that?" asked Ali.

"Because he never gets in trouble when Mike's here."

"Is that right?" She glanced at Mike and he shrugged.

As Ali entered the dining room, she gasped. Maria had prepared a veritable smorgasbord of Mexican cuisine. There were tortas, tamale, tacos, quesadillas, pambazos and a range of other dishes that Ali couldn't identify, but that looked and smelled amazing. Triggered by the colors and the aromas her stomach announced itself, loudly.

Maria pushed a full plate in front of her. "Mike, get some food in the woman before she starves."

For the next half hour Ali ate her fill of the amazing cuisine as she was bombarded with questions from Maria and the two boys.

"It's rude not to eat it all," whispered Mike as Maria ladled another serving of tamale onto her plate.

"Please Maria, your food is amazing but if I eat anymore, I'll burst."

"Nonsense, a skinny little thing like you should eat much more."

Thankfully, the ring of Maria's cell phone ended the

ladling of food. She excused herself and moved into the kitchen to answer it.

Ali spooned some of the food onto Mike's plate. " You've got to help me with this."

"Nooo, I can't eat anymore."

Maria reappeared, shaking her head. "Mike and Ali, I'm so sorry to do this but I've got to duck away and help out a friend."

Ernie rose from the table. "Is everything OK?"

"One of the girls is having a bit of a cooking crisis. Tomorrow she has a school baking day. I shouldn't be very long. Will you be fine with the boys?"

"Not a problem," said Ernie.

"Will you two still be here when I get back?"

Mike grinned. "If you promise to bring back some of whatever you're baking."

"Of course, darling. Ali, make sure you've got room for dessert."

Ali managed a sickly grin as Maria left.

Once she was gone Ernie gestured outside. "Well, I think we should head back out to the deck and catch the last of the sun."

"Do you want us to help clean up?" Ali asked as they rose from the table.

"No, we'll sort that later."

A moment later they were sitting in deck chairs drinking beers while the boys played in their sandbox.

"This is the life," said Mike as he relaxed. "Not a care in the world." As he spoke his and Ernie's phones started buzzing. He pulled it from his pocket and checked it. "You've got to be shitting me."

"What is it?" asked Ali.

"We've been recalled," said Ernie.

"Recalled for what?" she asked.

"Not sure." Mike placed his beer on a side table and rose. "We've got to report to the base. Ernie, do you need a lift?"

"I can't leave the boys."

"Yeah right, I forgot."

Ali stood and joined them. "I can watch them till Maria gets back. She said she wasn't going to be long. Then I can get a cab home."

Mike frowned. "You sure you're OK with that?"

"Yeah, I look after my nieces all the time."

"These two can be a bit of a handful."

"Oh please, they're four. What could they possibly get up to?"

He shook his head. "Don't ask."

As Mike backed his truck out of the driveway he shot Ernie a glare. "This is the test, isn't it? You're going to see how she fares with the boys." He dropped the truck into drive and took off toward the base.

"If she can manage those two after the amount of sugar they've had, she can handle anything."

"Sugar? Did Maria agree to this?"

"In theory."

"So, you told her about the Girlfriend Selection Course."

"Not exactly. In fact it was TJ who convinced her it was a good idea." He gestured to the side of the road. "Pull in here."

Mike brought the pickup to a halt behind a gray van and they got out. He followed Ernie who opened the side door revealing Rick in a camping chair, eating popcorn. "Hey boys, you got here just in time for the show."

The inside of the van was lined with monitors and there was a bench with a row of laptops. He recognized it as a surveillance setup. "Where the hell did you get this?"

"TJ borrowed it from a buddy with the Feds." Rick directed Mike to a chair. "Ernie and I spent the afternoon wiring the house for sight and sound."

Mike sat and watched the screens. Sure enough, they showed images from a half dozen cameras around the Ernesto residence.

"Your girl's got her hands full." Rick pointed at one of the screens.

The boys had abandoned their play in the sandbox and were now pursuing separate activities. Ryan was in the kitchen with the dog and James was on the dining room table pushing leftovers around with a toy bulldozer. Ali was frantically attempting to talk him down, while at the same time catching plates as they spilled off the end of the table.

"Damn, Ryan's a straight up mountain goat," said Rick. In the kitchen, the four year old had pulled out drawers and was using them to climb up onto the counter.

"Maria's going to kill you, and Ali's going to help her hide the bodies. Things are getting a little out of control," said Mike.

"This is nothing," said Ernie as Ali grabbed James off the dining room table, tucked him under one arm and searched for Ryan.

"All things considered, she's not doing too bad," added Rick. "I mean, they haven't started throwing poop yet."

Mike pointed at one of the screens. "What the hell is Ryan doing?"

The preschooler was sitting on the counter with his back

to the camera and was concentrating on something in front of him. Suddenly, a flame shot into the air above his head and he dropped a lit cooking blowtorch onto the floor.

Mike jumped from his chair. "Are you shitting me? I'm going back in there."

"Ernie, I think your dog's on fire."

Mike turned back to the screen and watched in horror as the Collie's coat ignited.

Suddenly, Ali appeared and extinguished the dog with a wet dishcloth. She recovered the burning torch, turned it off, and grabbed Ryan off the counter, in the space of a few seconds.

"She's fast, but not fast enough."

On another screen, James had climbed back onto the dining room table and was sliding through the remnants of dinner.

Ernie laughed. "Maria is so looking forward to them being big enough to help around the house. Something tells me this is not what she had in mind."

"Guys, seriously. This isn't funny. One of the boys could get badly injured."

"You kidding me? They're indestructible, *essé*. They'll burn the house down before they get hurt."

"And that doesn't bother you?"

"Ali's got it in hand, bud," said Rick. "See, she's got the boys under control... sort of."

She had the two boys outside now and they were running around on the lawn chasing the dog with a hose.

"Mike's right, Ernie. Maria's gonna kill you."

"Like hell. She said this was a good idea. I quote, 'I don't want Mike dating anymore of those vacuous, narcissistic, princess bitches." He imitated Maria's high-pitched voice perfectly.

135

"She said that, she actually said that?" asked Mike.

"Hey, you can't argue, it's true, buddy. That Stacey chick was hot as hell but damn, she was a selfish bitch," said Rick.

"Rick's right, *essé*. You've picked some *loco* women."

"Thanks guys, we've been over this, remember."

"The good news is this one's a bit of a kid whisperer." Rick pointed up at the screen where Ali had the boys sitting on the grass. She'd found a book and was reading them a story.

"That's impossible," said Ernie. "I jacked them up on so much candy they should be bouncing off the walls. Now they're eating out of her hand. Mike, don't let this one go. She is a goddess."

He managed a smile. "It would seem so. Well, I guess she passes this phase. Only one to go."

Rick shook his head. "TJ isn't gonna believe this."

"You know, if we head back now we might be able to clean the place up before Maria gets home," said Mike.

Ernie jumped out of his chair. "Good idea, you know what they say. 'A Happy wife, a happy life'."

Rick stuffed another fistful of popcorn into his mouth. "Nah, 'no wife, happy life'. You cats have fun, I'll see you at the beachfront tomorrow for training."

"You're such a dick, Rick."

"That's what she said."

Mike slammed the door of the van. "What are we going to tell Ali?"

"Same old story. False alarm," answered Ernie.

Chapter Sixteen

"I have to admit, Mike, that girl of yours is impressive," said TJ as he led the squad on a run along Coronado beach.

"That's what I've been telling you the whole time," said Mike as he avoided a patch of seaweed.

"Hey, let's not pin the trident just yet boys," said Rick. "There's still one more gateway."

Mike sighed. "What's that Rick, some kind of idiotic opportunity to cause her even more discomfort? You going to test her ability to carry five tons of shopping over an obstacle course?"

"Hey, that's not a bad idea. But no, this phase is all about pleasure. I call it the honey Rick."

Mike scowled. "The honey Rick?"

"Yeah, it's like a honeydick except…" He held his arms wide and pointed to his chest as he pranced through the sand.

"What the fuck is a honeydick?" asked TJ.

Mike shook his head. "The opposite of a honeypot."

Ernie grunted from the back of the squad. "You know,

how an attractive woman uses her sexuality to seduce a man and gain information. Well a honeydick is the male version."

"I know what a honeypot is, dipshit. Mike, Rick seems to think he's a goddamn lady slayer. So tonight he'll try to charm Ali."

"What!" Mike stumbled and almost fell. "And I'm supposed to agree to that?"

Rick turned and ran backward, facing the rest of the squad. He stripped off his tank top. "You afraid I might succeed? You afraid she might succumb to the body of Adonis?"

"I'd be more scared of Axe stealing her."

Rick flexed his arms. "Good thing she's a vet, because I'm going to be bringing out these sick puppies."

"Sweet beard of Zeus, that's bad." TJ gave the Rick a shove, sending him tumbling backward into the sand. "Mike, I think your girl's pretty safe. Let's get this last phase wrapped up so we can start planning the bachelor party."

As the squad trained Ali was finishing up a rehabilitation session with Axe. The dog now walked normally and showed no sign of his previous behavioral issues. She was immensely proud of what she had achieved in such a short period of time.

"Is that the stud's beast?"

Grinning, she glanced back at her sister who handed her a coffee. "Yes, it is. This is Axe."

Leonie sat on the grass. "He's a handsome fella, just like his dad."

"Yeah, we're almost ready to take him to the next level."

"You talking about Axe or Mike?"

She joined her sister on the patio as Axe stretched out at their feet. "Mike's in the dog house."

"Really?"

She shook her head. "No, not really. But, last night's dinner did prove interesting."

"How so?"

"Everyone got called away to an emergency and I was left looking after two hyped-up preschoolers."

"Worse than my two?"

Ali rolled her eyes. "The girls are angels compared to these two. Leonie, they set fire to the dog."

Her sister's coffee splashed, almost spilling on Axe. "Holy shit, that's serious. I tell you what girl, from the amount of drama that comes with this boy he better be hung like a rogue bull."

"Tell me about it. I feel like the first five dates have been some kind of test. Every time we're together I come up against some kind of obstacle or problem that I have to solve."

"Babe, that's just life. It likes to throw you a shitload of curve balls. You like this guy and he likes you. Go with the flow. It'll all work out in the long run."

"I'm just wondering what else life's going to throw at me."

"When's your next date?"

"Tomorrow night, we're going to a show in town."

"Well, that sounds pretty straightforward. I'm sure it will be fine."

"Yeah, we'll see. What are your plans for the day?"

"I was going to do some shopping then pick up the girls from preschool, excitement plus. What about you?"

"I've got a full day here, then I might have an early one."

"Shall we do lunch on Thursday?" asked Leonie as she rose.

"Yes, let's."

She kissed Ali on the top of her head and said, "You can tell me all about your date."

When her sister was gone. Ali leaned down and scratched Axe between the ears. "Well, handsome man, how about we get you inside for some breakfast?"

Once in the clinic she poured him a bowl of dried food and checked on two other canine patients. As she finished filling their water, the phone in her office rang.

"Hello," she answered.

"Is this Ali?"

The voice was familiar, but she couldn't place it.

"It's Ernie's wife, Maria."

"Oh, of course, I'm so sorry. I didn't recognize your voice."

"I'm sorry if this seems out of the blue. Ernie's mother had your number and I wanted to ring and apologize again for the other night."

Ali smiled, Maria was such a sweetie. "That's no problem at all. I'm just glad that we got everything cleaned up."

"You did an amazing job with the boys. They can be a real handful."

"They're actually very sweet."

"Yes, well you more than passed the test."

Ali frowned. "Test?"

Maria chuckled. "Yes, it was the boy's idea. You see Mike keeps dating the most inappropriate women. They thought it would be a good idea to see if you were family material. I stupidly agreed to their silly plan. Poor Mike didn't even know."

"I see."

"After meeting you last night. I know that he's in fantastic hands. You're divine, my dear."

"Thanks, Maria. And thanks again for a wonderful meal. I look forward to seeing you and the boys, soon."

"You too Ali, have a great day."

As she hung up a tsunami of anger crashed over her. Now everything made sense. The mountain hike, the sickness, and, most recently, the chaos with Maria's boys. They were running some kind of test to see if she was worthy of a SEAL. The sheer arrogance of it made her cringe.

What if she'd failed one of the tests? Would Mike have discarded her despite what they had? Hell, she hadn't dropped him when it turned out that he had financial problems. She shook her head in disbelief. How stupid was she? Mike probably wasn't broke at all. More likely, they had staged it all as part of their stupid selection process.

Reaching for her phone, she started to message him, then stopped. No, that was letting him off lightly. She tossed the phone on her desk and folded her arms. Failing the next test would be a suitable gauge of Mike's commitment. If he was willing to let a stupid test destroy what they had then it wasn't worth keeping.

The border guard took the stack of passports from Ramirez and checked them individually before handing them to a colleague. "You're all from Castle Insurance?"

"Yes, that's correct. We're all here for the big event in San Diego. We're pretty excited to be attending the fifteenth

Annual Home Insurance Conference." He handed the officer actual tickets to a conference that was being held in the city that week.

The officer checked the documents and handed them back. Then he peered in through the windows at the freshly-shaved men inside. All of them were dressed in dull business suits and wore bored expressions.

"The next one yours as well?" He pointed to the matching gray minivan behind them.

"Yes sir, there are twelve of us. We're the best in the company at what we do, that's why–"

"Sir, I don't give a shit how good you are at selling insurance. You just need to answer my questions. Then I can get you on your way."

"Yes, very good."

The guard walked to the second vehicle and inspected the men inside, along with their luggage, as the passports were processed. Once that was complete he handed them back to Ramirez. "Have a good time."

It was a short drive from the border crossing point to a quarry located a dozen miles from the outskirts of the city. Situated in an isolated valley the site was accessible by a single dirt track.

They parked the vans in front of a cluster of buildings that included the quarry's offices and equipment sheds. Ramirez stepped out into the dry hot desert air and surveyed the location through mirrored sunglasses. The metallic smell of crushed ore hung in the air.

The quarry made for a good ambush location. The access road entered the valley and crossed a large cleared area dominated by steep sides. Around the clearing were piles of gravel. There was a single front-end loader parked alongside a conveyor-fed crusher.

"Mr. Cortez." The voice came from the buildings.

His man in San Diego, Eduardo, was an unremarkable looking Latino who blended easily in a crowd. For that reason he was Ramirez's number one fixer.

"Eduardo." Ramirez shook his hand. "I trust everything is in order."

"Of course. It's all inside." His eyes narrowed as he watched the men alight from the two vans. "You brought a lot of guys this time."

He placed his hand on Eduardo's shoulder. "We're killing Navy SEALs, not gang bangers."

"Understood. I was able to find everything you wanted."

"Show me." He followed the man into the quarry's office. A smile formed on his lips as he surveyed his agent's work.

A map was stuck to the walls with locations marked by red pins. Around it were photos of a woman, a veterinary clinic and a quaint house with a picket fence. He pointed at the home. "Is this where she lives?"

"Yes. It's the best location, a long way from any police stations or military bases."

"Good. Show me the equipment."

"In the workshop." He directed Ramirez through a side door and into a large shed. Laid out on the floor was an arsenal of weapons and equipment, which included assault rifles, combat vests, two sniper rifles and half a dozen single-shot rocket launchers.

"What about the camera?"

"It's in the office. There is an internet connection and a laptop. All the gear is new and will be destroyed once we are done."

"And the bodies?"

"We have barrels of acid."

"You've done well, Eduardo. Show the men where they're staying. Then we'll conduct a reconnaissance with the kidnap team. I also want men providing continuous security."

"Yes, boss."

As his fixer went about his tasks, Ramirez returned to the office and studied the photo of the woman. The girl was pretty. He traced his finger across the photo. It would be satisfying to watch her die in front of him.

Chapter Seventeen

Ali felt the eyes of a dozen men on her as she walked into the Brassy Saloon. Her dress, a full-length, backless, black and white floral print, hugged her curves. And to ensure Mike got the message, she wore bright red lipstick, three inch, open-toed heels, and her hair hung loose across her bare back.

As she approached the bar a handsome black man in a well-tailored suit flashed a friendly smile.

She ignored him and took a seat.

"What are you having, gorgeous?" asked the bartender.

She smiled. "I'm waiting for someone. I'll order when he arrives."

He winked. "Lucky guy."

She felt her phone vibrate in her purse and fished it out. It was Mike. Here we go, she thought as she answered.

"Hey, babe. I haven't been able to get away from work yet. I'm going to be at least another forty-five minutes."

Ali shook her head. He actually sounded disappointed. "You know that's when the show starts?"

"I know, I'll meet you in the foyer. I promise I'll make it."

"OK, I'll see you then." She tossed her phone in her bag.

The handsome man moved to the seat next to her. "Your date running late?"

"It seems that way." She gestured for the bartender.

"Mine too. It sucks to be the dependable one. Seem to spend half your time waiting around."

"Tell me about it." The bartender appeared and Ali ordered a Manhattan.

"Make it two and let me get it," the man said.

Ali smiled. "No, I can't let you do that."

"Sure you can. You get the next one. I mean we've got an hour to kill till the show starts."

She managed a smile. "You're going to see the ballet?"

"Yes, I am." He extended his hand. "My name is Richard."

"I'm Alison. It's a pleasure to meet you, Richard." As she shook his hand she noticed how well he was dressed. He wore a finely cut gray suit with a light blue shirt, opened at the collar. On his wrist was an Omega, similar to the one Mike wore.

"So Alison, are you a local or a visitor to our fine town?"

"A local, I run a small veterinary clinic out at Iron Canyon. What about you?"

"I'm in banking. Well, I used to be in banking. I'm semi-retired now. I sit on a few boards, but most of the time I write."

"Really, what sort of writing?"

The drinks arrived and Richard paid for them. "Oh, a bit of poetry and the like. Nothing serious. Just dabbling really. Do you have any artistic pursuits?"

"Not really, my work takes up most of my time."

"I guess when you have a job as important and fulfilling as helping heal animals you don't need a hobby."

Ali smiled. She was enjoying talking to Richard, not that she believed he was a retired banker. She'd joined the dots quickly, the coincidence of him being at the bar, the Omega watch and the name Richard. On Mount Otay Mike had blamed his illness on his team-mate, Rick. This had to be another stupid test. And if that was the case then she was going to run with it. Plus, even if he was acting, Rick was a good listener and seemed genuinely interested in what she had to say. They ordered a second round of drinks and before they knew it forty-five minutes had passed.

Ali rose and made to leave. "I guess your date hasn't made it either."

"She's notoriously unreliable. A good friend, but not one for timings. Do you mind if I walk with you?"

"That would be lovely." The idea of arriving with the handsome Rick appealed to her. It was a short walk from the bar to Spreckles Theater, where the ballet was showing. The Chicago-style building was over a hundred years old. A marquee over the entrance displayed the performance name in bold, black letters on a white background.

As they reached the doors Richard smiled. "Would you like me to wait with you?"

"If you like, it would be nice to introduce you to Mike." She pulled out her cell and checked the time. He was already ten minutes late. The phone buzzed as a text arrived.

I'm so sorry I can't get away. Enjoy the ballet and we'll grab a bite to eat after.

Glancing up she saw Richard watching her. "Bad news?" he asked.

"Mike can't make it. I guess I'll be watching the show alone."

He checked his watch and frowned. "No, we can't do that. Look, Clarissa is clearly not coming and I've got director's circle tickets. Join me."

"Thank you, but it wouldn't be right."

"Alison, I simply wish to enjoy the ballet in the company of a new and interesting friend."

"Alright, but first let me send Mike a reply."

Richard waited at a respectful distance as she typed a response.

Don't worry. I'm going to head straight home after the show. I will see you tomorrow.

The performance lasted nearly two hours and Ali watched in rapt attention. Her gaze never left the dancers as they twirled to the notes of a full symphony orchestra. When it was finally over she sighed and slumped back in her chair.

"That was amazing," said Richard.

"It was, wasn't it."

"I think it was made even more enjoyable due to the company. You should have seen your face."

"It was delightful. I really wish Mike could have been here."

"His loss, I'm afraid."

They waited for the crowd to thin before leaving the theater.

"Would you like to get a nightcap? There is a great little bar not far from here."

"No, I'm afraid I'm feeling a little worn out. I'm going to head straight home. Thank you so much for a wonderful evening, Richard."

"My pleasure. Look, Ali, I wouldn't usually do this but I was wondering if I could give you my number."

"Richard, you're an amazing guy but I'm already seeing someone."

"I understand. Well, I have had a fantastic time. Thank you again, Alison." He pecked her on the cheek.

Ali smiled as she turned and walked away. It had been a lovely evening despite Mike's absence. That thought reminded her. She still needed to fail the test. Turning she chased after Rick. "Richard!"

He turned. "Yes?"

"Your number. I changed my mind."

She registered the look of surprise on his face followed by what could have been a glimmer of sadness. Then he managed a smile. "That would be fantastic. He took a card from his wallet and handed it to her. Give me a call anytime."

She took the card, found a pen and scribbled her number on the back. "How about you call me tomorrow."

Rick watched her walk down the street and hail a cab. Then he turned and strolled slowly in the opposite direction. A block further along the road he ducked into a pub and sat next to Mike. He placed the business card on the bar.

Mike stared at it for a few seconds before he picked it up and crushed it in his fist.

Ali sat in the back of the cab staring at her phone.

A few minutes into the trip the driver glanced at her in the rearview mirror. "You don't look happy, Miss,"

"I'm not. I just found out my boyfriend has been secretly testing me to see if I'm worthy."

"And that upsets you?"

She narrowed her eyes at him in the rear-vision mirror. "No woman would be happy with that."

"That's the difference between men and women. A man would see it as a challenge. Whereas, a woman might see it as a man not loving her for who she is."

"Exactly."

"So, did you fail on purpose?"

Ali frowned. "How could you know that?"

"Lady, I've been married for thirty years and that's exactly what my wife would do."

"Yeah, well that is exactly what I did."

"And now you're hoping he'll call you anyway."

She sighed. "Yeah, I guess so."

"Well, if he loves you he will. Now, this is you." He pulled the cab up in front of her home.

She paid and tipped him before stepping out onto the grass curb and kicking off her heels.

"Good luck," said the cabby through the window as he drove off.

As she was about to walk up her drive her phone vibrated and she glanced at the screen. It was a message from Mike.

Hey, I'll be around tomorrow to pick up Axe.

"Message received loud and clear, Michael Saunders," she murmured fighting back tears as she began to write a text.

Mike, sorry your little tests didn't go to plan. I will see you tomorrow.

She didn't see or hear the gray minivan as it stopped on the street. Staring at her phone she reread the message, wondering if he was as hurt as she was. Maybe she should let him stew on it for a few more minutes before she hit send. Fumbling with the lock she opened the door as she heard footsteps on the gravel behind her.

Turning, she called out in a loud voice. "Who's there? Mike, if this is another of your stupid tests…"

She caught a glimpse of two masked men then suddenly they were on her. A hand clasped her mouth as she was lifted from the ground by strong arms. The keys slipped from her grasp, as she struggled. Her heels fell off. A hood was slipped over her head plunging the world into darkness.

Chapter Eighteen

Mike sat in his truck outside the clinic, contemplating how best to handle Ali. He felt betrayed, but also disappointed. She had fooled him. She was just like all the other women he had dated, always looking for a better deal.

Now, he had to decide how to end it. Hell, she hadn't even replied to his text about Axe. Finally, he climbed out of the truck and entered the clinic.

The assistant behind the counter greeted him with a smile. "Are you here to see Axe?"

"Yeah, I'm here to take him home."

"Oh, in that case I'm going to have to call Ali."

Mike checked the clock on the wall. It was nearly ten in the morning. She should have been at work hours ago. "Does she have the day off?"

"No, she just hasn't been in yet." She lifted the phone to her ear. "That's weird, it's not connecting."

"Try her home number."

She dialed again and waited. "No one's answering."

Mike frowned. Was it possible she'd taken his text to heart and was avoiding him? No, that wasn't like Ali.

"Hey, how about I take Axe and go around and check that she's OK?"

The assistant shrugged. "I can't see a problem with that. I'll grab him for you."

As Mike waited, he tried using his cell to call her number. It immediately went to voice mail.

The assistant handed him Axe's lead. "Here he is."

The dog barked loudly and immediately sat next to Mike's leg. "Good boy. Hey, can you email through my final bill."

"Sure, I'll do it now."

As they left the clinic, Mike was amazed at Axe's strength. He moved as if he had never been injured. No matter what he thought of Ali, her skill as a vet was undeniable.

Axe jumped into the truck with ease. A moment later, they drove through Iron Canyon and headed to Ali's suburb. As he pulled into her driveway, he spotted the open door. He sprinted from the truck and almost tripped over a pair of heels. Her keys and purse were next to them. "What the hell."

Checking the garden, he found no sign of her. He slipped inside and quickly searched every room. Nothing. She wasn't avoiding him. Someone had taken her.

———

Ramirez sat at a desk in the quarry office, drumming his fingers against the chipped laminate surface. His kidnap team had returned with the bait. Now he needed to set the trap.

Eduardo stuck his head through the doorway. "Boss, she's ready for you."

"About time." He followed the fixer into the equipment shed through to one of the quarry's storerooms. Inside the woman was tied to a chair on a sheet of plastic facing a camera on a tripod. Ramirez gestured to the armed guards. "Is she really that dangerous?"

"She keeps trying to escape."

Chuckling, he stood in front of her and tugged the hood from her head. What greeted him was not the terrified victim he expected. Instead, he faced the fierce glare of a woman enraged.

"Where is Mike?" she snarled.

"Your boyfriend? You will see him soon enough."

Her eyes darted around the room. "What are you guys supposed to be, Mexican gangsters?"

Ramirez frowned. "We are not supposed to be anything. I don't think you understand the gravity of this situation."

"I don't think you understand the gravity of this situation, buddy. I'm over this shit and I'm over Mike. Get him in here now and I'll tell him myself."

Ramirez dropped the hood back over her head and gestured for Eduardo to join him outside. "What the hell is she talking about?"

He shrugged.

"It doesn't matter." He took his phone from his pocket and dialed Barbosa. The cartel boss answered after a few rings. "You wanted to know when we had the girl."

"Excellent, call me once you have the SEAL and I will make sure I'm at the computer."

He terminated the call. "Are the men in position?"

"Yes, they are ready."

SEAL of Approval

"And her phone?"

He reached into his pocket and produced Ali's cell phone. "They turned it off like you asked."

"Good, but now we want Mike Saunders to know exactly where she is." He powered up the device, stepped back into the storage room and tore the hood off his prisoner's head. "What's your password?"

"Why don't you ask Mike? I'm sure he already knows it."

He clenched his fists. "I'm not screwing around. Give me the password."

She laughed. "Why, so you can see if I called that guy from last night? Is this some final test to see if I'm worthy? You know what, fine. The code is two-three-six-seven. Oh, and Mike, if you're listening, I think you're a pathetic, misogynist asshole."

Ramirez unlocked the device. On the screen was a text message. He smiled as he read it out loud. "Mike, sorry your little tests didn't go to plan. I will see you tomorrow."

Ali cocked her head to one side. "See, I worked out your little game."

"I guess you won't mind if I hit send then." He transmitted the message as he left the room and waited. Seconds passed before the phone rang. The name Mike was displayed on the screen.

"Ali, I just got your message. Look, I want to apologize." The man's voice was edged with concern.

"Listen to me very carefully, Mike Saunders," Ramirez growled.

"Who is this? Look if you've—"

"Shut up and listen. We have the girl and if you want to see her again come to the Atlas Quarry, alone. If you bring

155

anyone with you, she dies. If you call the police, she dies. If you are not here within the hour, she dies. Come alone and she will live." He terminated the call, turned off the phone and handed it to Eduardo. "The trap is set."

Chapter Nineteen

Mike skidded his truck to a halt outside of the team building and sprinted inside, leaving Axe in the cab. Reaching his locker he grabbed his low-profile body armor and stuffed it in a gear bag. As he turned to leave, he locked eyes with TJ who was sitting on a bench seat working on paperwork.

"Mike, you OK, brother?" asked the Chief.

For a split second he contemplated not telling TJ. But the squad was his family and if anyone knew what to do it would be TJ. "No. Some Mexicans grabbed Ali and they want an exchange in…" He checked his watch. "Forty-five minutes."

"Exchange for what?"

Mike sighed. "Me. It has to be linked to Barbosa's brother. This is the revenge the Lieutenant briefed us on."

TJ pulled open his locker and grabbed his gear. "Right, and they gave you a deadline?"

"Yeah, an hour. Don't call the cops and come alone."

TJ slipped into his rig. "Motherfuckers don't know who they're messing with."

Rick entered the room with Ernie. "Who doesn't know?"

"No time to explain. Grab your gear and meet me at the armory."

"We got a job on?" asked Ernie.

"Yeah, I'll explain on the way. Mike, you got a location?"

He held up his phone. "Atlas Quarry, only ten miles away. It's got high ground all around it."

"Rick, you're on the sniper rifle," said TJ as he ducked out of the team room.

Three minutes later Mike pulled the truck in front of the armory. TJ had already unlocked the secure building. The boys grabbed their weapons and climbed into the bed of the pickup with Axe. TJ tossed in a bag of preloaded magazines they kept for contingencies and joined them, securing the cover.

"OK, let's do this," he broadcast over the secure radios they wore.

Mike checked his watch as they sped across the causeway that linked Coronado to the mainland. They had thirty minutes to make the timings dictated by Ali's kidnappers. Flooring the accelerator, he sent the truck screeching around a corner.

"Steady, brother," transmitted TJ. "I'm trying to study Google earth back here and come up with a plan."

"We've got a plan," said Mike. "We're going to kill them all and rescue Ali."

"Good plan. I'm keen to flesh it out a little."

"Well you better hurry because we've got less than half an hour to get there."

Ramirez sat smoking, watching the clock on the wall above the woman's head. Uneasy, he switched between the clock and studying his captive. The woman still believed this was all some kind of test that her boyfriend had organized. Why he would do such a thing baffled him. "Do you still think this is a game?" he asked, exhaling a stream of smoke into her face.

She coughed as her eyes darted from the armed guard in the corner of the room to the camera set up on the tripod.

"Your boyfriend, Mike, killed someone important to my client. Someone he loved dearly. Because of that, he has asked to watch Mike lose someone close to him. Unfortunately, that someone is you."

He watched as realization set in followed by mounting panic. "You don't understand. He won't come. He thinks I wanted to cheat on him."

"He will come. I sent him your angry little message." He laughed as she struggled against her bonds. Then, somehow she managed to tip the chair over backward. There was a loud crack as her head struck the concrete.

"Shit." He leaped to his feet. The last thing he needed was for her to die before the target arrived. "Get her upright," he barked at the guard.

The man grabbed the chair and yanked it onto its legs. Her head lolled forward against her chest.

Ramirez checked her vitals. She was breathing and had a strong pulse. Inspecting the back of her head he found a rapidly expanding lump. She would live, for now.

The sound of the door opening caught his attention.

"There's a truck approaching."

"Is it him?"

"Our snipers have confirmed there's only one person in the vehicle."

"Good. Let's go out and meet him." He turned to the guard watching over the woman. "Make sure nothing happens to her."

On his way out of the equipment shed Ramirez drew his pistol and checked it was ready. Then he joined the four men waiting to provide him with security. The rest of his people were already in their ambush positions.

Mike slowed the truck as he drove through the gates at the quarry. A battered sign read, *Atlas Resources*. He inched the truck forward, scanning the terrain for any sign of an ambush.

"Rick, you got anything?" he asked through his earpiece. They'd dropped him on a back road with access to the hill behind the quarry. He'd sprinted to get into position in time to cover their arrival with his sniper rifle.

"Negative," he managed between breaths.

"OK, we're going in." He drove the truck into a clearing in front of a cluster of buildings. Stopping in line with a huge ore crusher, he opened the door and stepped out into the dust.

Dry, hot air assaulted his senses, sun reflecting off the sheer rock walls of the quarry. Through his sunglasses he spotted movement. "We've got five tangos pulling CPP on a single primary. Gotta have at least a sniper pair in overwatch." His lips barely moved as the five men escorted a single, seemingly unarmed individual dressed in a suit and aviator sunglasses. As they got closer Mike identified he was Latino, they all were. There was no doubt about it. They had to be the Butcher's men.

"Rick?"

"I've got eyes on one sniper, looking for others."

Mike glanced at the high ground dominating the quarry then focused on the men. "Where's the girl?" he yelled.

Aviators stepped forward. "She's inside. Surrender yourself and I'll release her."

"Like hell!" yelled Mike. "You bring her out here and show me she's alive. Then we'll talk about what happens next."

The man laughed as his security detail aimed assault rifles at him. "The way I see it, you're coming with us, no matter what."

"Taking down the first sniper," reported Rick.

Mike thought he caught a glimpse of movement high on the lip of the quarry as he raised his hands. "Fine, I'm coming."

"Target down. I'm going for number two," said Rick.

Suddenly a shot rang out from high on the quarry wall. A bullet shattered the windshield of Mike's truck.

"Shit, sorry guys," said Rick. "Fucker got a round off. He's neutralized."

As Mike dropped to a knee, he whipped a pistol from the back of his pants. Blasting away at the group of men he saw one fall before the others returned fire. He sprinted for cover. Bullets churned the dust around him

From the back of the truck, Ernie and TJ appeared, their carbines spitting lead.

Axe leaped from the bed onto the gravel and dashed to Mike's side as he found cover behind the gravel crusher.

"Covering," Rick reported from the crater wall above them.

Ernie slid in next to Mike, tossing him a spare carbine and assault rig. It took him a second to throw it on then they fired in the direction of the buildings as TJ sprinted toward them.

"What the hell happened with Rick?" Mike asked as he shrugged on the rig. "Is he OK?"

"Yeah, when he nailed the sniper, the prick got a shot off," said TJ. "We've got to fight through before they kill Ali."

Ernie returned fire then yelled, "That's going to be a problem. We're outnumbered." A volley of bullets clanged into the crusher sending the men ducking for cover.

"Rick, what have you got?" TJ transmitted.

"I'm taking heavy fire, guys. I'm going to have to move. We've taken out three guys. I think there's at least ten more."

More rounds hit the crusher forcing them further back. Mike searched for Axe but couldn't find him anywhere. "Guys, have you seen Axe?"

"Negative," responded TJ.

"He was here a second ago," said Ernie.

For a second Mike forgot the raging gun battle and searched for the dog. He was nowhere to be seen. Clearly he was still suffering from PTSD, because despite being trained to work in a gunfight, he'd run away.

"Team," TJ's gruff voice snapped him back to reality. "We need to flank these fuckers. Mike, can we climb up through the crusher and over that mound of rubble?"

Mike peered up through the rusted steel beams. "Yeah, but that's going to take us further from the buildings. That's where they'll be holding Ali."

"It's our only option, bud. If we stay here we're going to be dead and of absolutely no use to her."

Mike clenched his fists in frustration. "I'll lead."

Chapter Twenty

Ali's heart raced as the sound of gunfire echoed through the flimsy walls of the storeroom. She fought the tape that held her arms to the chair. By wriggling her fingers she'd managed to loosen the bonds, ever so slightly. Thankfully, the boss with the sunglasses hadn't replaced the hood and she could see, albeit barely. The blow to the back of her head had left her with blurred vision and a splitting headache.

Suddenly, bullets punched through the thin sheet metal to her left. She screamed, toppling the chair over and onto her side. Her heart felt like it would explode as she fought her mounting panic.

The door opened. A blurry figure entered. She assumed it was the guard. She felt his hands grab her shoulders and push her back upright. "Don't move, bitch."

At that moment, she spotted a second, smaller shape at the doorway. A shape she knew well. His low guttural growl filled Ali with hope.

"Axe, it's you?"

She flinched as he leaped toward her. The guard screamed as Axe slammed into him. His weapon clattered to the ground. He fought back but Axe's attack was brutal. As Ali's vision finally cleared she saw the guard dash from the room, his mauled arm dangling uselessly.

"Good boy, Axe."

The dog nuzzled her then sat next to her, watching the door like a hawk.

Ali worked her taped wrists back and forth, managing to loosen them enough to free one hand. Then she pulled the tape from the other. Gunfire still raged outside as she stripped the tape from her legs, wincing as it tore her skin.

Barefoot, and still wearing her dress from the night before, she padded across to the door and peered out. No sign of her guard, she spotted a number of gunmen firing out toward the quarry. There was an enormous front-end loader parked in the shed, obscuring the others.

"Where do we go, Axe?"

The dog led her out through a back door and away from the gunfight. He followed the shed before stopping at a corner. Ali made her way cautiously over the gravel and stopped alongside him. "Hey, we need to get out of here, buddy."

Axe whined as he stared intently in the direction of a rusted ore crusher. Ali spotted Mike's shattered pickup a short distance away.

"He's out there, isn't he?"

Axe's eyes never left the crusher.

"If we go out there we're dead, Axe. But, there might be another way. Come on, boy. Let's see what we can do."

"RPG!" yelled Mike when he spotted a plume of smoke spiraling out from the enemy position. The rocket screamed toward them and slammed into the pile of concrete drainage pipes they were using as cover. It exploded, showering them in dust and shrapnel. He felt a searing burn on his upper arm as hot steel sliced through his shirt.

"Everyone good?" bellowed TJ as he jumped to his feet and returned fire.

Mike checked his wound. "I'm good."

"I can't see shit," reported Ernie.

Mike registered the sound of another rocket launching. It streaked away from the equipment sheds and detonated high up on the cliffs. "Rick, you OK, buddy? That was a bit too close for comfort."

"Guys," Rick's voice was weak. "I've been hit. I've taken some shrapnel to the leg. Bleeding badly. Gonna try to get a tourniquet over it."

Mike turned to TJ and took in his grim expression. "We better call 9-1-1. We can't do this alone."

"Agree. We're pinned here. Without backup they're going to–" Another rocket exploded against the cement pipes. "-Pick us off one by one." He pulled out his phone and made the call.

Without Rick's covering fire the barrage hitting their position intensified. Mike tried to get a shot off but nearly lost his head as bullets snapped past inches away.

"TJ, Mike, Rick, I want you to know that it's been an honor serving with you. You're my brothers. And if we go down here, I'm proud it's with you," said Ernie.

"Fuck that," yelled Mike. "We're not going out like this." He leaned out from the pipes and fired full automatic in the direction of the sheds. "We can make a break for the office buildings."

"Negative, Mike," yelled TJ. "We wouldn't make it ten yards. We sit tight and wait for the cops."

"And what about, Ali?"

"Mike, if she's still alive, us running out there and getting killed, isn't going to help."

"She's alive, TJ."

"I don't doubt that, bud."

Mike fired another burst. He heard yelling coming from the gunmen.

"Ammo check!" yelled TJ.

"Two mags," replied Mike. "And, I think they're forming up for an assault."

"I've got two and a half," said Ernie.

"I've got two and Rick's out of the fight," confirmed TJ.

Mike didn't need him to outline exactly how dire the situation was. Their only hope was that the police arrived in time to turn the tide of the battle.

Ramirez knew he had the SEALs on the ropes. With their sniper down the rest were pinned behind a stack of concrete piping. He'd moved up with his men and was using a cluster of shipping containers to command the assault.

"Bring up the remaining rockets," he commanded Eduardo. "Have three of the men fire on them from here. The others will assault from the right flank. We need to move quickly before the authorities arrive."

Men dashed forward to their new positions. Then Ramirez waved them on with his pistol. The men providing covering fire unleashed a hail of bullets and rockets that smashed into the concrete piping. Ramirez grinned as he pictured the SEALs cowering, while his assault force leapfrogged from cover to cover on the flank. In a matter of minutes, they would be on top of the Americans.

He felt his phone vibrate in his pocket and he checked the screen; it was Barbosa.

"I've been sitting in front of this computer for ten minutes!" the Butcher screamed.

"There's been a change of plans. The SEAL brought friends," Ramirez yelled over the gunfire.

"You better kill them all or you're dead!"

Ramirez gritted his teeth. "For all of them the price has tripled." Barbosa didn't need to know that he had every intention of killing them for free.

"Fine, but I want evidence. I want photos of them and the woman too."

The girl, Ramirez had forgotten all about the girl. "It'll be done." He terminated the call and turned to his fixer. "Eduardo, kill the girl. Get photos."

"Yes, boss."

He turned his attention back to the battle. His men were less than a hundred yards from the Americans now. Soon it would be over. He'd abandon the team and slip away before the police arrived.

"Boss!"

At Eduardo's panicked scream, he glanced back at the equipment sheds. He heard a rumble and froze. The massive front-end loader plowed through a cloud of diesel smoke. A second later the mechanical monster gained speed and swung toward them. "Shit!" It was the woman behind the controls. As he raised his pistol the bucket lifted, blocking his shots. Diving to one side, he managed to avoid the wheels as it rumbled past.

The men firing on the SEALs were fixated and didn't see it in time. The blade lowered smashing them into the shipping containers, crushing them. Then the tractor backed off the wreckage and turned toward his assault force.

Ramirez fired his pistol into the back of the cockpit to no effect as it trundled forward. Screaming with rage, he ran after it, ducked between the wheels, grabbed the ladder to the cab, and started climbing.

———

"You hear that?" Mike yelled. The rate of fire from the cartel gunmen slackened as the rumble of a powerful diesel engine echoed off the quarry walls.

He peered around the crumbled concrete pipes but couldn't identify the source of the noise.

TJ and Ernie joined him as he spotted a group of gunmen forming an assault line. "They're trying to flank us," he said firing the last of his ammo at the men. The Mexicans dove for cover as two of their force were hit.

Mike dropped his carbine and snatched his pistol from its holster. "I'm out."

"Me too," added Ernie.

The gunmen retaliated, unleashing a hail of gunfire. Then, sprinting forward in pairs, they began assaulting, using piles of gravel for cover. Mike fired his pistol, to no effect. Just when he thought it was over, the diesel engine's noise intensified. A huge front-end loader smashed through the rubble, sending the gunmen scattering in all directions.

As the earthmover turned toward him, he spotted Ali at the wheel. She was handling the twenty-ton juggernaut like a seasoned pro. He spotted a figure at the top of the access ladder; it was the aviators wearing boss. Raising his pistol, he took aim. "Damn." He couldn't get a clear shot.

A rifle blasted close to his head. He caught a glimpse of one of the shooters toppling over.

"Get your hands up!" TJ screamed at the remaining men.

Mike ignored them as he sprinted after the earthmover. Out the corner of his eye he spotted a gunman aiming at him and flinched. The man went down.

"I've got you, brother," Rick said softy, over the radio.

Gaining on the front-end loader, he saw the cartel killer wrench open the door and aim his pistol. Then a flash of fur and teeth hit him, knocking him from the ladder. Man and dog plunged between the massive tires, disappearing in a maelstrom of dust and smoke.

"Axe!" Mike screamed as the earthmover came to a shuddering stop.

Heart pounding he peered under the earthmover, into the dust.

Ali appeared from the cabin. "Mike, is he there? Tell me he's alive."

As the dust dissipated Mike spotted a mangled and bloodied corpse. "Oh god, no."

A whimper cut through the air. Axe appeared, bloodied, battered and covered in soil.

"Axe, buddy, are you OK?" The dog walked toward him and licked his face. Mike wrapped his arms around him. "Yeah, you did good boy, you did good."

Tears streaming down her face, Ali stepped off the ladder and limped across to them. "Is he hurt?"

Mike turned to her. "He's fine. How are you?"

She nodded, smearing the tears from her face with her hands. "Battered and bruised, but overall, good. Is everyone else OK?"

"Rick got hit. It's bad."

The wail of sirens filled the air and a helicopter roared over the quarry. Mike turned and watched as a police SWAT van skidded in the gravel. Black-uniformed officers swarmed from the vehicle, their weapons aimed at the few remaining gunmen who had already surrendered to TJ and Ernie.

"Looks like the cavalry arrived just in time."

More police cars arrived, followed by a fire engine and an ambulance.

"Guys, if you're not using those paramedics I could do with a hand," transmitted Rick over the radio in a weak voice.

"I'm on it," replied Mike.

"Negative, we've got this. You take care of that girl," TJ said as he and Ernie trotted past with medics in tow.

Mike turned back to Ali. Barefoot, clad in last night's torn and filthy dress, with diesel soot smeared across her face, she'd never looked more beautiful to him. "Do you think you could bring it upon yourself to forgive me?"

"For ditching me last night or your childish selection course?"

He grimaced. "Both."

For a split second, her jaw clenched and he thought she would slap him.

"You know you're an idiot, Mike Saunders?"

He nodded. "Yeah, I know."

"You don't have to do everything your team-mates tell you to do. Sometimes you can trust your own instincts."

"They meant well."

Ali glanced up at the quarry wall where TJ was over-seeing the movement of Rick back to the ambulance.

"They're good guys, Mike, and so are you."

He grinned sheepishly. "So, does that mean you like me?"

She shook her head. "You're such an idiot. I've known about your crappy test since yesterday morning. Maria called and let the cat out of the bag. I also worked out that Richard was the Rick you blamed for the food poisoning. Oh, and you both wear the same watch. Pretty slick operation you're running, not." Her eyes narrowed. "When I found out I literally wanted to kill you."

"But, now?"

The kiss surprised Mike. She stood up on her tiptoes and despite his assault rig and rifle, landed it directly on his lips.

As she pulled back, he clasped her close and deepened the kiss. Their mouths still locked he swept her off her feet and into his arms. "We need to get you checked out. You've been through a lot."

She laughed. "Really? You think after your crappy selection course I'm going to be phased by a kidnapping and a gunfight?"

"No. You're probably pretty well prepared for anything now. But this is for my peace of mind." He carried her through the gathering crowd of vehicles to a newly arrived ambulance and sat her on a stretcher. A paramedic immediately began inspecting her for injuries.

TJ and Ernie appeared carrying Rick on a stretcher. Bloodied and battered with a bandaged wound to his thigh he still wore a grin.

"Hey Ali, sorry, I was meaning to call."

"Hello Richard, how's the poetry going?"

"You know, hit and miss." He gave Mike thumbs-up as they loaded him in the ambulance next to Ali.

Mike frowned. "So you failed on purpose?"

She nodded.

"Why?"

The paramedic dabbed at the wound on the back of her head and she flinched. "Because I was angry. I let you into my life, Mike. I got to know you. And, you still wanted to run me through your stupid tests."

"Ma'am, I need you to lie down. You've suffered a concussion," said the paramedic. "We need to get you to hospital and have it checked out."

Mike nodded. "It was pretty stupid."

"Yeah, it was."

The paramedic grasped her shoulder. "Ma'am."

"Fine."

As she lay Mike climbed into the back and Axe jumped in after him.

"Sir, we can't have a dog in here."

Mike shrugged. "Sure, but you're going to have to tell him that."

The paramedic took one look at Axe's teeth and relented.

"You guys really like me, don't you?" Ali grinned.

Mike tucked a stray hair behind her ear. "I can't speak for Axe. But I can say... I've fallen for you."

Chapter Twenty-One

Mike knelt in front of Axe and looked the dog directly in the eye. "Buddy, this is probably going to be our toughest gig ever. Yeah, I won't lie. It's going to be brutal. It's going to be tough. We've trained for unconventional warfare. We've fought cartels and terrorists. But this is going to take it to the next level."

Axe cocked his head to one side as if he understood exactly what Mike was saying.

"I know, brother, I'm scared as well. But we've got to do this. I mean come on, you're a decorated war hero."

Ali walked into the living area of her sister's house and stood with her hands on her hips. "Are you boys hiding in here? Come on team. You've got thirty screaming preschoolers out there and they want Mike the clown and his circus dog, Axe."

Mike sighed, rose and adjusted his costume.

"Come here, honey, you've smudged your face." Ali took the theatrical paints from the coffee table and used scarlet to outline his mouth. Then she adjusted his red nose and rainbow-colored wig. "There, now you look the part."

She glanced down at Axe. The dog was wearing a rainbow colored ruffle around his neck and had tiny bows in his fur. "You look very cute as well, Axe." She tousled his ears. "Well boys, this is only day two of husband selection, so get out there and charm those princesses."

"Surely this makes us even?"

"Not even close, lover. Now get rolling."

Mike grabbed a basket filled with treat bags and walked slowly through the sliding doors, into the backyard, with Axe at his side.

As thirty satin-clad, wand-waving fairy princesses spotted them, their screams hit him like a blast from a sonic weapon. An army of over-excited Disney characters, they descended upon the pair, demanding balloons, magic, and candy.

Mike held them at bay with the treat bags, but Axe wasn't so lucky. Girls swarmed all over him, pulling his ears and aggressively patting him. The Military Working Dog took it in his stride, sat calmly and looked up at Mike with eyes that said, why?

Deep in the folds of his costume Mike felt his phone vibrate. He fished it from his pocket and checked the screen.

Butcher located-rolling in 30.

He dropped the basket and made a beeline for the house. Safely inside, he stripped off the clown outfit revealing shorts and a T-shirt. His wig was tossed onto the lounge along with the red nose.

"Where do you think you're going?" demanded Ali from the kitchen where she was enjoying a coffee with Leonie.

"I've got a job on."

"Barbosa?"

He nodded.

"Go get him, honey."

As he made for the front door he heard the rattle of claws on the wooden floor. Glancing over his shoulder, he saw Axe had followed him. The dog sat and tipped his head, his lopsided ear flopping forward.

"You want in, don't you?"

Axe let out a sharp bark.

"OK, come on."

"Just remember, the selection process isn't over," yelled Ali from the kitchen. "I'm not saying yes till you pass all five stages."

"Maybe we'll stay in Mexico, hey Axe," he mumbled.

"I heard that." Ali appeared and wrapped her arms around him. "Be safe."

He kissed her, smearing red paint on her mouth. "I will. Axe has my back."

"You look after each other."

"That's what we do."

Chapter Twenty-Two

"Cut-off is in position," reported TJ as he crouched next to Mike and Axe. The squad had parachuted into an area close to one of the Butcher's many haciendas. It was still a few hours before dark and they hid in the thick vegetation surrounding the home.

"And intel's still got him in location?" asked Mike.

"Correct," reported Ernie. "They've got multiple sources confirming his presence."

"Then what are we waiting for?"

"A green light from command," said TJ.

"He's going to slip away again."

"No he's not," replied Ernie. "We just got our green light. We're on point. Bravo and Charlie are backup and we've got snipers in position."

"Mike, you and Axe have lead," ordered the Chief. "Let's take him down, for Rick." The Corpsman was still in hospital.

"For Rick." Mike stepped out of the bushes with Axe by his side. TJ and Ernie followed, and behind them, the rest of the platoon. He moved quickly across the freshly mowed lawn, his weapon held ready.

Rounds snapped through the air as snipers engaged the guards on sentry around the facility.

Mike made it to the front door and tested the handle. It was unlocked. Pushing it open he slipped inside. "Axe, hunt."

The dog made a beeline for the staircase to the second level as the rest of the SEALs cleared the ground floor. Mike and his squad followed the dog.

Upstairs, Axe stopped before a doorway, staring intently at it.

Mike sniffed. The scent of tobacco hung thick in the air. Music blared loudly from down the hallway. He waited for TJ to tap him on the shoulder before swinging into the corridor.

Two cartel guards standing ten yards away saw him. They went for their guns. It was the last move they made. TJ and Mike dropped them with silenced shots.

Axe worked his way down the corridor before halting at another doorway. Rock guitar blasted from behind the thick wooden paneling.

"This is it?" asked TJ.

"Yeah. Axe looks pretty excited."

"OK, let's do this."

Mike scowled as he turned the handle of the door and pushed it gently open. The music increased in intensity as he peered through the gap.

The room inside was lavish. Through the haze of smoke he spotted a large bed. A naked woman sat astride an overweight male with her back to him.

Mike smirked, reached out and killed the stereo.

"What the fuck!" Barbosa pushed the girl off him.

Sitting up he spotted the two SEALs. "No, no, don't kill me!" he screamed as he stared wide-eyed at Mike.

At Axe's low vicious growl, the girl screamed. Wrapping herself in the sheets she stumbled from the bed, leaving the naked cartel boss cowering.

"No, not the *payaso*. Not the *payaso*," he sobbed. "Not the *payaso*."

"Cover me," TJ grunted. Lowering his weapon, he flipped the naked man onto his stomach and flexi-cuffed his hands behind his back. "Find something to cover this turd."

Mike tossed him a robe from the back of the door.

They escorted the cartel kingpin to the front lawn where Commander Conner waited with a Blackhawk helicopter. He greeted them with a broad smile. "Job well done, guys." He frowned at Mike. "You come straight from a party or something?"

"Yes, sir. A kid's birthday party." He frowned. "How did you know that?"

The Commander winked and gave the dog a nod. "Good to see Axe back in the field."

The loadmaster grabbed the senior officer by the shoulder, informing him that prisoner had been loaded.

"OK boys, we need to get this guy to the FBI. I'll see you back at the strand."

The Blackhawk powered into the sky leaving them to wait for their own ride.

Mike turned to Ernie. "What's a *payaso*?"

"A clown."

"Why would the Butcher scream that when we captured him?"

TJ and Ernie stared at him with raised eyebrows.

"Have you seen your face, Bobo?" grunted TJ.

179

Ernie handed him his smartphone with the camera flipped. "Who knew the butcher is afraid of clowns."

Mike glanced at the screen and saw that he was still wearing most of the stage makeup that Ali had applied. "You guys could have said something."

A Blackhawk thundered into view and flared onto the lawn.

"Where's the fun in that?" yelled TJ as they climbed onboard. "Plus, Ali scares the crap out of us and we promised her we wouldn't interfere with the selection process."

Mike shook his head as he secured Axe's harness to a strap. "You do know that you guys got me into this mess."

TJ gave him thumbs-up. "Yep, but goddamn it's been worth it."

As they lifted off, Mike reached down and ruffled Axe's ears. "Yeah, I guess it has."

The dog rested his head on his thigh.

Mike sighed. "I can't wait to see what Ali's got lined up for us next."

Next in the SEAL Series

vinci-books.com/seal-the-deal

A bachelor party turns perilous for a Navy SEAL and his canine companion.

Navy SEAL Mike Saunders and his loyal canine companion, Axe, face overwhelming odds during an epic bachelor party gone awry in the backwoods of Oregon. As an unlikely hero emerges to save the day, love blossoms in the midst of chaos.

Turn the page for a free preview…

SEAL the Deal: Chapter One

Jennifer Reynolds leaned against the hood of her Ford pickup and sipped from a banana, acai and mango smoothie. Tall with a slim athletic build she cut an attractive figure in the khaki and green uniform of an Oregon Parks and Recreation Department Ranger. Her pale blue eyes watched the road out of town from beneath a felt campaign hat. Not one for sunglasses she tended to squint. Which, combined with her upturned nose, full mouth and high cheekbones, gave her a country girl next door look.

A passing pickup tooted its horn and Jenny, as her friends called her, raised her hand and waved. Oakridge, Oregon born and bred she'd left the small town after high school to pursue a career in law. Ten years later she was back having abandoned a corporate salary to pursue her childhood dream job.

As she finished the smoothie an SUV pulled out of the parking lot behind her and stopped alongside. The window lowered revealing a blonde woman in her late fifties.

"Hi Darlene," said Jenny.

"Afternoon, darlin'," replied the woman in a southern drawl. "Is class still on at five?"

Jenny nodded. "Yeah, but next month it changes to six. Sam is switching up the rosters."

Darlene smiled. "Don't you go canceling on us. Those classes are just the dandiest. I've got two new girls comin' along tonight."

"The more, the merrier."

"I haven't felt this fit since I was running track at Oklahoma State." She leaned out of the window and whispered. "And, ever since I got that home pole, Steve and I have been at it like jackrabbits."

Jenny laughed.

"No, seriously. It's done wonders for my confidence. I never thought pole dancing could be so therapeutic."

"I'm glad to hear that."

The radio on Jenny's equipment belt crackled. "Reynolds, you there?"

She recognized her boss Sam's voice. "Darlene, I have to take this."

The woman waved. "I'll see you tonight."

Jenny watched her drive away as she lifted the radio to her mouth. "Sam, Reynolds here."

"Jenny, can you shoot over to the Country Club. They've got a bear stuck in one of their dumpsters."

"Again? Seriously boss, do they ever fasten them?"

"Clearly not. Brian says it's only a little fellow. You'll be able to handle it, right?"

"I'll get over there right now." Jenny stowed the radio and climbed inside the pickup.

She grinned as she drove through the sleepy town and out onto the 58 toward McCredie Springs. A year ago she'd been part of a takeover of a multi-million dollar company.

Now, she was speeding through the rolling tree-covered hills of Lane County to rescue an overly inquisitive black bear. She'd always dreamed of being a park ranger, but she'd been swept up in the pressure to attend college and join the corporate world. Long hours, dealing with endless greed and a failed relationship had been the catalyst to move home and pursue that dream.

The McCredie Springs Country Club was located on the outskirts of the Willamette National Forest, the one and a half million-acre park that Jenny helped manage. Technically it was outside of her jurisdiction, but when it came to wildlife that didn't perturb rangers.

She left the highway and drove along a pine-lined lane and into the opulent grounds. White colonial style villas dotted a landscape of vines, woods, golf greens and fairways. The heart of the estate was a southern mansion that housed the restaurant, day spa and offices. Turning off the main road she passed the swimming pool and stables, heading toward the equipment sheds.

A hundred yards out she spotted one of the bright green police cruisers of the Sheriff's Department. Two uniformed officers were talking to Brian Douglass, the property manager. She parked a distance away and walked across to join them.

She recognized the officers; Ed and Harold had attended the same high school as her, albeit a few years later.

"Well if it ain't Jenny the bear wrestling lawyer from New York." Ed was the mouthier of the two. His hulking partner Harold didn't say much.

Jenny ignored the jibe and approached the manager. "Hi, Brian."

He gave a warm smile. "I'm sorry, Jenny. One of the

staff forgot to fasten the latch. Came out here this morning and found the little fella inside." He gestured to a large dumpster positioned under a tree. "These boys were passing by, but they haven't been much help."

Ed spat in the dust. "Come on, that ain't right. I offered to shoot the damn thing."

Jenny glared at him as she walked across to the dumpster. Lifting the lid she peered inside. A snarl startled her and she dropped it with a clang. Instinctively her hand moved to the butt of the pistol she wore on her belt.

Ed laughed. "What's wrong Jenny? You scared of the little bear?"

Harold laughed.

Jenny exhaled and lifted the lid again.

In the bottom of the steel dumpster sat a young black bear. She guessed its weight at a little over eighty pounds, most likely a female. The shredded remains of trash bags surrounded the animal. It had evidently climbed in looking for food and couldn't grip the smooth sides to get out.

She flipped over the lid triggering aggressive roars from the bear. "Brian, I think it might be the same one as last time."

"Yeah, I figured as much. Once they work out where the food is they keep coming back."

Jenny strode to the bed of her truck where there was a large metal cage. She dropped the tailgate and hefted the cage to the ground. Then she grabbed a pole with a cord on the end of it and a long piece of two by four. "I'm going to relocate her to the park."

Brian took the timber from her. "Good idea. I'd hate to have to destroy her."

Ed watched from a distance. "Be easier to shoot it.

There are plenty of bears in the park and this is a nuisance animal."

Jenny fixed him with an icy look.

"Hey, if I want to shoot it I can. This is Lane County jurisdiction, not National Forest."

She gestured for Brian to join her at the bin. "Shoot it, Ed. See what happens if you do."

"Don't threaten me, Missy," growled the deputy.

She turned to him and smiled. "That's not a threat, it's a promise. You try and destroy that animal and I'll push this pole sideways up your ass." A jiggle of the noose emphasized the point.

Ed scowled and Harold chuckled.

"Shut up idiot," he snapped.

Jenny turned her attention to the bear. "Brian, drop that log in so she can climb it."

The rancher followed her instructions and a moment later the head of the bear appeared over the lip. Jenny hooked the noose over its head and pulled the animal to the ground. Then with Brian's help, she maneuvered it into the transportation cage.

Ed watched from a safe distance, hand resting on the butt of his pistol.

"Don't just stand there. Help us lift the damn crate onto the truck," bellowed Brian.

The deputies helped out but didn't hang around for long. With the bear secure they continued their patrol, leaving Brian and Jenny sharing a Bud Light.

"Useless as all hell. Don't know why the administration staff called them," said the former rancher.

Jenny finished her beer and tossed it in the dumpster. "Well, this little lady shouldn't give you any more trouble." She checked her watch. "I've got enough time to get her back to the station, tagged and out into the park." She climbed into her truck.

"Till next time," Brian shot through her open window.

"Keep those bins closed."

"Yes, ma'am."

Jenny unwrapped her legs from the floor to ceiling pole and lowered herself slowly to the ground. "OK ladies, last move," she shouted over the pumping music.

Around her a dozen women dressed like her, in crop tops and leggings, attempted to replicate the move to varying levels of success. When they had all touched down she killed the music.

"Well done, a great effort by everyone. Let's run through some stretches and wrap it up."

She'd been instructing the small class at a dance studio in Jacksonville for the past six months. In that time it had grown from a few friends to classes of up to twenty women. Word had spread fast. If it continued she was going to need a bigger premises.

Once the warm down was complete Jenny pulled on a pair of track pants and a hoodie.

"Another fantastic session," gushed Darlene as she made to leave.

"You've really progressed," she replied, tying her laces.

"Like I said, getting a pole at home was a smart move."

"Jenny, when are you getting more portable poles?" asked another of the women.

"Yeah, I want one too," added another.

Grinning she grabbed her gear bag. "They should arrive

later in the week. I'll update my Facebook page as soon as they're in."

She left the dance studio and crossed the parking lot to where she'd left her car. On her way she spotted a massive truck parked alongside her Chrysler. A tall figure leaned against the door of a shiny new Ford F-150 Raptor.

She recognized Lieutenant Carter Brown by his trademark Stetson hat and square stubble covered jaw. Dressed in jeans, boots and a check shirt he wore a pistol on his belt. He was the senior officer at the Oakridge Sheriff's station and a former classmate of Jenny's.

He tipped his hat as she approached. "Miss Reynolds, how are you this evening?"

She managed a tight-lipped smile as she took out her keys. "I'm good thanks, Carter."

He stepped away from his truck. "Jenny, look, I dropped by because I wanted to apologize for the way my men acted today. Old man Douglass rang my office and gave me a heads up."

Jenny turned to the handsome police officer and shrugged. "It was nothing. Boys will be boys."

He laughed. "True, but I would like to make it up to you by taking you out to dinner."

"That's a lovely gesture, Carter, but totally unnecessary. I appreciate the courtesy of a face-to-face apology. Thank you, from one professional to another."

He took a step closer and placed his hand on the car door. "Look, all I'm asking for is dinner. We'll grab a steak, my treat. It'll be good for intra-agency relations."

Jenny put her key in the lock. "In that case, you should drop by the ranger station and catch up with Sam and the rest of the crew. Bring Ed and Harold, we'll put on coffee and donuts."

A scowl split his granite features. "I'm not someone you want to make an enemy of."

"No one's trying to make an enemy of you, Carter. I'm just declining your invitation to dinner. As far as I'm aware, that's not a declaration of hostile intent."

"You threatened one of my officers today. I could bring you in for that."

She turned to face him with hands on her hips. "Really? You're going to arrest me based on a flippant comment that was made in jest." She held her wrists out. "Take me in, big shot. I'll take great pleasure in destroying your fantasy in court."

"Just watch yourself, Jenny."

She smiled. "I will."

He turned, opened the door of his pickup and climbed in. The rig rumbled to life and he backed clear before roaring off down the road.

Jenny frowned as she watched the Ford disappear. The Raptor was an expensive truck. Not something a police wage would easily buy. Pushing the thought from her head she climbed into her sedan. She needed to get home, feed her cat, put dinner on and get to bed. The team had an early start in the morning.

A dozen miles out of Oakridge a battered pickup with a bloodhound in the bed was parked beneath a tree on a dirt track. Two men sat inside. Hank, the older of the two, wore jeans, a denim shirt, battered cowboy boots and a ten gallon hat. Carl wore woodland camouflage pants and a stained USMC T-shirt.

Hank held a cell phone to his ear. "Yeah, no worries

we'll get it done." He ended the call and slid the phone into his shirt pocket. Pulling a revolver from his belt he popped the chamber and checked it was loaded.

"So, what's the deal?" asked Carl.

"Travis reckons he's been stealing dope and selling it on the side."

"Shit, that's low. Real low." Carl took out his Glock pistol, cracked the slide and eyeballed the brass cartridge in the chamber. "He want him dead or fucked up?"

"Smith's got kids. So, just a few broken bones to get the point across."

Carl smirked, holstering his pistol as he pulled an extendable baton from the pocket of his combat pants. "Been waiting to try this sucker out."

Hank frowned as he started the truck. "Where the hell did you get that?"

"I bought it online. Got me a sweet deal on a whole bunch of stuff."

"More useless military junk." He dropped the pickup into gear, turned on the headlights and planted his foot on the accelerator.

The truck bounced along the rutted track its lights illuminating thick woods on either side. After half a mile they passed a fence, turned right and stopped in front of a rundown farmhouse.

"I'll handle this. You back me up," said Hank as he killed the engine and donned a pair of thick leather gloves.

"Why am I always the backup?" whined Carl.

He turned with a frown. "Because you're a goddamn fuck up." Climbing from the truck he strode toward the house. As he approached the door opened and a figure clutching a shotgun appeared in the porch light, Andrew Smith.

"Who's out there?"

"Hey, it's Hank and Carl," Hank said as he climbed the steps to the porch, fists clenched by his side.

Smith relaxed and lowered the shotgun. "Oh, hi guys. Thought you might be rustlers. Someone tried to steal some gear outta my barn the other night."

Hank nodded. "Seems to be a lot of that going around." He swung a savage right hook as he reached out and ripped the shotgun from Smith's hands. His fist caught the man on the jaw and he went down like a sack of potatoes.

"Nice punch," said Carl as he joined him.

"Help get him around behind the barn." He lifted the unconscious man by one arm.

Carl took the other and they dragged him past the truck out of the light cast by the porch and behind a dilapidated barn.

They sat him against a wall and Hank slapped him. "Wake the fuck up."

It took a moment for the man to come to. When he did, he tried to climb to his feet. Hank jammed the revolver under his chin. "Sit tight, boy."

"What's this all about?" the man stammered.

"Why don't you tell me?"

Smith stared across at Carl with pleading eyes. "Look, I haven't done anything wrong, I promise."

"That's not what Travis is saying."

The fear dropped from his face, replaced with a look of contempt. "That fat fuck's a liar. What the hell has he told you?"

"Said you've been stealing dope," added Carl.

Hank turned and silenced his partner with a glare. Then he turned his attention back to Smith. "Leg or arm?"

"What?"

He clenched his jaw and hissed through his teeth. "Leg or fucking arm."

Smith stared him in the eye. "You'd take Travis's word over mine?"

"Carl, do both." Hank stepped back, his pistol still aimed at Smith's face.

"Really? You mean it?"

"Just do it."

His partner flicked the extendable baton from his pocket and stepped in over the top of Smith.

"Carl, we've been friends for a long time—"

The sickening crack of his leg snapping cut him off. A blood-curdling scream filled the air as Carl lifted the baton and smashed it into his arm, crushing more bone.

Hank pushed his partner out of the way. "Shut the fuck up. Shut up or I'll shoot you in the goddamn head."

Smith managed to clench his jaw and stifle his cries.

"You see that, Hank? You see that? Barely had to swing the bastard. Did all the work for me."

He turned to his partner. "Shut the hell up and get the truck." Waiting till his partner disappeared he leaned in close. "You tell anyone who did this and you're dead."

The man nodded with his jaw clenched.

"Andy, where are you?" a female voice called from the farmhouse.

"You've paid for your transgression. Things are square. Don't do anything you or your family is gonna regret."

He shook his head. "It wasn't me, Hank."

Hank left him whimpering against the barn strode across to the truck and climbed inside.

"That was fun," said Carl as they drove back down the track.

"You're a sick fuck," he murmured as he took a pinch of chewing tobacco from a tin and stuffed it into his lip.

"Goddamn thief deserved what he got."

"So we're told."

Carl turned to him with a confused look on his face. "If he hasn't been stealing the dope, who has?"

Hank spat into an empty coke bottle. "How the fuck would I know?"

SEAL the Deal: Chapter Two

The beat of rotor blades penetrated the Plexiglas windows of the cockpit and reverberated through Mike Saunders' chest. The square-jawed twenty-nine-year-old wiped his hands on his knees. His palms were sweaty despite the frigid air inside the helicopter. He glanced out the window at the snowcapped mountains and exhaled slowly.

A Navy Special Warfare Operator, the grey-eyed SEAL was a veteran of two major campaigns and a dozen covert operations. He'd spent hundreds of hours in helicopters flying over mountains, jungles, deserts and the ocean. However, never in his career was he ever this nervous. The plan was elaborate. There were so many things that could go wrong.

"How you doing bud?" asked the pilot over his headset.

He raised an eyebrow at the man and gestured over his shoulder at the other passenger.

"You're all good. She can't hear us."

"What's our ETA?" asked Mike.

"Couple more minutes. The guys on the ground have

everything ready. They're standing by for your arrival." He made an adjustment to the aircraft's controls. "So relax and stop looking so damn nervous." He nodded ahead. "OK, we're coming up on our landing zone."

Mike looked through the windshield at the approaching landscape. A boulder-speckled glacier between two high peaks rapidly approached.

He glanced over his shoulder at the passenger in the rear. Ali's green eyes sparkled from inside the hood of a North Face jacket. She wore a broad smile on her elfin features.

"Wow," she mouthed.

Her expression went a long way to easing his nerves. He and Ali had been dating for over a year now. In fact, for the last two months they'd been living together. Mike had never felt this way about anyone. He was totally and utterly in love with the beautiful veterinarian. She was intelligent and kind, but also independent enough to deal with his military career. What's more she adored his dog, Axe. This holiday to the South Island of New Zealand was his way of thanking her for everything she had done for them both.

Smiling he turned his attention back to the terrain ahead. The glacier loomed and a moment later the pilot touched the skids down on the hard packed snow, killing the turbine. "OK kids, this is it. Welcome to the Franz Josef glacier."

Mike stepped from the cabin, opened the rear door for Ali and surveyed the surroundings. Snow-capped mountains stretched out in every direction. In the distance, he could see the coastline and bright blue Tasman Sea.

"It's stunning, babe," she murmured.

Feeling her arms around his waist he turned, wrapped

her in a hug and kissed her. The view lost its magnetism as their lips touched.

A moment later they parted and Mike turned to see the pilot at the nose of the helicopter pretending to inspect the windshield. He looked up, saw they were done and smiled. "OK, lovebirds. If you come with me, I'll show you the best view this side of the equator."

As they followed him across the glacier toward a rocky outcrop Mike's keen eye spotted fresh tracks in the snow. He glanced sideways at Ali; her attention was fixed on the horizon. She turned to him, grinning like a child at Christmas. Then she frowned and cocked her head. "Mike, can you hear that?"

He took her hand. "No, what can you hear?"

Her eyes sparkled. "Music."

Mike's pulse quickened as they rounded the outcrop and the notes of a violin reached his ears.

"You're kidding me." Ali stopped dead in her tracks and squeezed his hand.

A pair of deck chairs sat in the snow. Between them was perched a silver champagne bucket beside a platter of fruit, cheese and caviar. A few yards away a violinist dressed in a tuxedo was playing.

The pilot gestured to the chairs. "Please, take a seat."

Ali sat and the pilot turned waiter, placing a blanket over her legs. Then he poured them each a glass of champagne before disappearing behind the outcrop.

Mike turned to Ali and raised his glass. "To the most incredible person I know."

A tear formed in her eye as she lifted hers. "You're so sweet." She gestured to the view. "This is unbelievable."

His heart raced as he glanced at the violinist. The man nodded and changed the song.

It took a moment for Ali to recognize the tune. "That's 'My Heart Will Go On'." She turned to the musician.

Mike felt like a squadron of butterflies would burst from his stomach as he reached into his pocket. He slipped out of his chair, took her hand and knelt.

Her eyes went wide as he raised the velvet case and snapped it open. "Alison Charlotte Taylor," he said with a waver. "Will you make me the happiest man alive and marry me?"

Tears filled her eyes and she nodded. "Yes, yes. Of course, I will."

As he slipped the diamond ring onto her finger, she leaned forward and kissed him. Their lips touched and Mike felt all the anxiety of the last twenty-four hours replaced by elation. He was going to be marrying the love of his life.

Grab your copy...
vinci-books.com/seal-the-deal

About the Author

Jack Silkstone grew up on a steady diet of Tom Clancy, James Bond, Jason Bourne, Commando comics, and the original first-person shooters, Wolfenstein and Doom. His background includes a career in military intelligence and special operations, working alongside some of the world's most elite units. His love of action-adventure stories, his military background, and his real-world experiences combined to inspire the no-holds-barred PRIMAL series.

About the Authors